THE MALTESE DAHLIA

Paul Vincent Lee

Spirit Aid is a humanitarian relief organisation dedicated to alleviating the suffering of children and young people whose lives have been devastated by war, poverty, genocide, ethnic cleansing and all forms of abuse.
The charity is based in my home city of Glasgow, Scotland and was started by a fellow East End Glaswegian; the actor David Hayman.

Perhaps because of that link; Spirit Aid is close to my heart, and a contribution from every one of my book sales will go to the charity.

Please visit www.spiritaid.co.uk to see the wonderful work done by the charity......and hopefully make a donation.
Thank you.

"Like slavery and apartheid, poverty is not natural. It is man-made and it can be overcome and eradicated by the actions of human beings."

Nelson Mandela

THE MALTESE DAHLIA
Copyright © Paul Vincent Lee 2014
Visit: www.paulvincentlee.com

This novel is a work of fiction. Any references to real people, living or dead, real events, businesses, organizations, and localities are intended only to give the fiction a sense of reality and authenticity. All names, characters, places, and incidents are either the product of the author's imagination or are used fictitiously, and their resemblance, if any, to real life counterparts is entirely coincidental.

First published in Great Britain by: Weeryan Ltd 2015.

Printed and bound in Great Britain by Lightning Source UK.
Printed and bound in Malta by Salander Group Co Ltd 2015.
Paul Vincent Lee asserts the moral right to be identified as the author of this work.

A catalogue record for this book is available from the British Library.

ISBN: 978-0-9572399-4-4

For my two wonderful sons: Anthony, who always supported me... even though he knew I was "aff ma heid" and Paul, who told me my writing "was getting better"... praise indeed.

Foreword

Some of the scenes featured in this story may make some readers feel uncomfortable and to possibly question how my own mind works. The truth of the matter is that the details are taken from actual cases and Post Mortems and confirm the view held by many people involved in law enforcement that what happens in reality is far worse than what any novel writer can imagine.

Paul Lee was privately educated in Glasgow by Jesuit priests, and he has successfully fulfilled their view of him as "someone who will never amount to anything."

The Maltese Dahlia is his second novel in the Inspector Thea Spiteri series and is set on the Maltese Islands, where he now lives.

THE MALTESE DAHLIA

Dahlia: *a showy flower with roots that form tubers.*

Tuber: A swelling on an organ or other body part

CHAPTER 1

Kapitlu

September/Settembru 2014
Morning/L-ghodwa

Angelica Senderos cursed herself as she jogged along the dusty tracks surrounding the fields outside Msierah. She passed the ancient Cart Ruts site and headed towards Tal Balal. She intensified her cursing as she thought of how stupid she had been, just a few hours earlier, when she had taken a pill from her newfound friend, Chloe, in the White Line Club.

Her body clock had stirred her from her bed at 7.30 a.m. as always and set her on her daily routine since arriving in Malta to study English a few weeks earlier. But on this morning, Angelica Senderos was unsure if she was jogging, in a trance, or still asleep.

Come on; get those legs and arms pumping, focus, concentrate. What's that? Fuck, I hope it's not a cat. Ignore it, focus, look straight ahead. No, something's not right, out of place.

The crimson trickle, seeping out from the swaying strands of golden wheat on her right-hand side, seemed surreal in some way. She stopped. The buzzing of flies drew her gaze further into the field. She pushed some of the crop to the side. *Run, Ang, run... don't look back... ever.*

***

Inspector Thea Spiteri, of the Maltese *Pulizija* homicide squad, had seen a number of dead bodies. Children, youths, adults, old people, male, and female; but she had never seen one cut in half. The sight of the young woman's body didn't repulse her; it was more a case of fascination.

The young Swiss girl who had found the body was standing propped up against a *Pulizija* rapid response team car. She had a distant, blank look on her face and an unlit cigarette in her hand even though she didn't smoke. Spiteri felt sorry for her; she had only questioned her briefly, then said that if there was anything else she needed to ask her, she'd get in touch. She put her arm on the girl's shoulder: 'I'll see that you get back to your flat okay.'

Two officers from the Rapid Intervention Unit and one District *Pulizija* officer seemed to be as equally dazed as the young girl. One of the Rapid Intervention Officers had told Spiteri that Senderos had frantically flagged them down, almost collapsed in front of their vehicle, in fact. They'd arrived at the scene within minutes of being told what the girl had seen. 'At first, it didn't look as if it could actually be a body. Not one at least; as the parts weren't connected. Close to each other, but somehow not. It's the worst ever, Mam. On Malta, anyway.' Spiteri had been confused initially but understood when she went to look for herself. Even in the bright sunlight, the corpse looked to be a wax model, a mannequin. The look was compounded by the fact that the body didn't seem to be lying in a recognizably human position. The attendant flies and beetles told Spiteri that this was no mannequin, and the clothing ... *expensive, but discreetly so...* indicated human remains even though little else did.

The Maltese Dahlia

The body itself had been decimated. The woman's face and breasts had been slashed and stabbed multiple times. Her vagina had been obliterated; stabbed and slashed so many times, it was now no more than a mass of masticated pulp lying on the woman's thigh. The two parts of the body were positioned exactly half a metre apart with the arms over the head and the legs in a V shape. Some of her internal organs had clearly been removed, but her liver and spleen were still visible. But perhaps the most disturbing aspect of the display was that the woman's cheeks had been sliced from mouth to ears on both sides; she appeared to be grinning. Spiteri also noted the rope marks on her wrists, feet, and neck. *She wasn't killed here. Christ, the press will have a field day with this.*

Spiteri turned to Detective Sergeant Sarah Said. 'What do you think?'

'Well, overkill like this usually means a relative has done it, but...'

'I know what you mean, but no... this killing is a message: "Look at me with awe, I am spectacular!" Was it raining last night?'

'No, I don't think so.'

Spiteri pointed over to a black coat and black umbrella lying a few metres from the body. 'Try and find out the last time it was raining around here.'

'Okay, but how do you know she was killed around here?'

'I don't, but we have to start somewhere.'

Both officers stared for a few more seconds at the mess that had once been a living person.

'He'll do it again' whispered Said.

Spiteri took a deep breath

'Let's go. I don't think we need to wait for confirmation of death, do you?'

The two officers turned and walked back towards Spiteri's car.

A voice from behind the *Pulizija* cordon shouted, 'Inspector, any comment for *The Independent?*'

Spiteri replied over her shoulder, 'Yes, we'll try our best not to be incompetent.' Old wounds never healed.

***

Afternoon/Waranofsinhar

Thea Spiteri was sitting in her office. She wondered if she had become immune to death over the last year. The site of the mutilated corpse had affected everyone who had seen it; except, seemingly, her. She had just finished a call to *Pulizija* Commissioner Kevin Galea, a man she had always liked and admired and had grown to respect even more over the last troubled year of her life and career. As an inspector, Spiteri was answerable to her Superintendent, who in turn reported to an assistant commissioner. Spiteri followed the chain of command, but always also made direct contact with Galea. Theirs was a link forged over the years through a mutual sense of trust and respect.

Galea had asked if she was alright about leading the investigation. Spiteri appreciated his concern; after all, it was only a few months since she had cradled the body of her own murdered lover in her arms—her soon-to-be husband, his head almost severed from his body by one of her fellow officers. The colleague was someone she had considered to be a friend as well as a trusted colleague at one time.

Spiteri forced her thoughts into the present. She looked out into the squad room, her squad now, with two new officers in place, one to replace the colleague who had killed her lover, and one to replace a female officer whose grief over the death of her child had driven both her and her husband into an eternity of madness.

Detective Sergeant Sarah Said was still in place and showing great promise. She had now been joined by newly promoted DS Dario Grimoldi and DC Michael

The Maltese Dahlia

Sammut. Spiteri had already instructed them to try and find out who the dead girl might be, to check missing persons or anything else they could think of. She watched as the officers sat at their desks, sifting through reports, occasionally lifting the phone; she knew it was a thankless and, she suspected, a futile task. Her own phone rang. She instantly recognised the cheery voice of Professor Paul Sammut, Head of Forensics and father of her new DC, Michael Sammut.

'Thea, I've completed the post-mortem, such as it is. Would you like to come over?' asked the professor.

'Yes, I'll be right there.' Spiteri rose and walked into the squad room. 'Sarah, PM results.'

The morgue in Mater Dei Hospital is surprisingly large for a small population such as Malta. Sammut often remarked that the size was necessary to accommodate the brain power present; even after many years, he still laughed at his own wit. On this occasion, however, there was no humour, not even the black humour that often helped people associated with death to cope. Both halves of the mutilated corpse lay on the same table, close together, but the small gap still visible between the two halves still made it difficult for the brain to take in exactly what it was looking at. A label—Body 6 A—was tied around the right wrist of the corpse; a second label—Body 6 B—was fixed to a toe on the bottom half. Spiteri had never seen that before and suddenly felt an overwhelming sadness for the girl.

Professor Sammut cleared his throat and started speaking, but in a voice that Spiteri noticed was quieter than normal. 'It's difficult to determine how long she's been dead. For example, I can't take a rectal temperature, but I'd say two days. The good news, if there is such a thing, is that nearly all of the major wounds were inflicted after death. Again, it's difficult to say, but I would say that the probable cause of death was the blows to the head. The bad news is that she was definitely tortured before being dispatched. I'd say she's about twenty-five years old. I measured from the top of her forehead to the top edge of the bisected torso, then from her heel to the bottom edge, round about the third vertebrae. I'd say she was quite small, around one-point-five metres, about fifty-two kilos.' The doctor stopped for a moment and looked up at Spiteri. 'It's the worst attack on a woman I've ever seen. I've taken prints and DNA samples; they're already away. I knew you wouldn't want to waste time.'

'Thanks, Paul' said Spiteri.

'Any thoughts on who would do this kind of thing, Professor?' asked Said.

Professor Sammut slowly shook his head. 'A maniac... if she was a prostitute, an angry client... who can tell? Most murders are committed by family, relatives, friends, as you know, but this...'

Spiteri's thoughts flashed to her former lover, a Scottish detective who had stated often, and loudly, "The victim knows the killer." Spiteri's sadness seemed to engulf her.

'Paul, in case the prints or DNA don't tell us anything, can you stitch up her face? Even at that, we can't put a photo out. Sarah, call for a sketch artist to come down here. Warn them in advance and tell them to do the best likeness they've ever done, but leave out the scars.'

Spiteri glanced back at Body 6 as she left the Lab. *Don't worry. I'll find out who you are; you won't be called that for long.* She would be right about that, but not in the way she imagined.

***

Night/ Serata

No one who had been directly involved in the day's trauma spoke of the event to anyone who had not been. There seemed to be an unspoken understanding that something had happened that day, on a tiny island in an idyllic setting... and that life would never be the same again. They were right.

Thea Spiteri lay on the top of her bed. She had already drunk one bottle of wine and, although she knew she needed to be up with the sun in the morning, she was halfway through a second. Her thoughts swirled in her mind. Her life seemed to have been split into two parts: pre- and post-2014. Pre- she had been, if not happy, then content. Her career had possibilities. She felt she had a good and loyal squad. She had a life-long friend and confidant in a Dominican priest who lived on the island. She had a lovely home and no financial worries. Life was good, but...

In a couple of months' time, 2014 would be over... and she was now neither happy nor content; merely empty. Her trust in her squad had been badly misplaced, her soulmate had proved to be the Devil... and the man she was to marry around this time was dead. She lay back and thought of her lost love. She smiled at the thought of the ranting he would no doubt have done when he heard that his beloved homeland, Scotland, had just voted "No" to Independence. Her smile evaporated and the tears came... as they did every night.

Professor Paul Sammut, too, lay on the top of his bed. Thankfully, his wife now slept in another bedroom in order to escape his "trapped bull" snoring. It wasn't just the horrific post-mortem he had performed that was concerning him. Something his son, Michael, had said to him a couple of days before was niggling away at the back of his mind. He prayed he was wrong.

CHAPTER 2

Peter Abela was a man who was permanently frustrated. He was now forty years of age and knew that he would never fulfil his dream of being a doctor. He was not a stupid man—a First Class Honours Degree in Accountancy and an MBA proved that—but no matter how hard he had tried, the mysteries of chemistry, physics... the sciences remained beyond his grasp.

Born in Gharb, on Gozo, his father had lost an arm in a farming accident when Peter was eight years old. The family had regularly visited the nearby shrine at Ta Pinu, where the young boy was fascinated by the crutches and prosthetic limbs that adorned the walls of the corridors behind the altar. His parents knelt and prayed, thanking God for his blessing allowing his father's accident not to have stopped him being able to work their farm. The fact that God could have prevented him from losing the arm in the first place didn't seem to be something his parents ever considered. The boy spent most of his spare time dissecting animals, birds, fish... anything he could get a hold of, and he liked nothing better than watching his mother gutting rabbits to make his favourite stew.

Peter Abela's faith was long gone, but his passion for all things medical remained and, once accepting that he would never be a doctor, he did the next best thing and made his career in hospital management. He knew he was good at his job and was passionate about providing the best service possible to the people of Malta in his role as Chief Executive of the new, state-of-the-art national hospital, the Mater Dei Hospital in Msida, and he had now surpassed even his own ambitions by recruiting a rising star of the international medical world after the two had met at an International Medical Conference in London and thrashed out a deal in two days; an appointment that would put Mater Dei at the forefront of transplant and prosthetics medicine and bring in much-needed revenue to the hospital.

***

Rex Wayne was a film nut. So, when his only son was born, it was obvious that there could only be one name for the boy: John... with the inevitable result of the boy being called Duke from an early age. Doctor Duke Wayne was well on his way to becoming the most talked-about surgeon in the medical transplants field. People had been a little surprised that he had decided to leave the United States and go to work in Malta, but the offer to start off and then head up a complete new department at the Mater Dei Hospital had proved to be too good an opportunity to turn down. His only slight concern was that it might be more difficult to get replacement limbs and organs when required, but his contacts and influence were such that he was confident he could overcome any issues. Another bonus was the fact that Malta had plenty of cinemas, as a passion for films was just one of the things he realised that he had inherited from his father; one of the good things, at least.

Young John was at college before he realised that the way his father treated his mother wasn't the norm. Yet, somehow, he blamed his mother for staying and grew closer to his father. Sylvia Wayne died after apparently falling down the stairs of their Texas farmhouse. John

The Maltese Dahlia

Wayne never got to find out that he was the reason she stayed.

***

Thea Spiteri did not have much time for the press as a rule, but Daphne Arrigo was the exception to the rule. Daphne had helped Spiteri deal with some difficult situations that had arisen in a series of complicated cases earlier in the year and the two had become friends. Both women had a lot in common: both single, no children, no parents, few friends... career women, on the surface at least. Daphne was now the Head Investigative Journalist with *The Malta Times*, and Thea smiled when she saw her name displayed on her mobile.

'I wondered how long it would take you!' said Spiteri.

'That's an awful thing to say, Inspector. I resent the implication. I was merely calling to see if I could take you for lunch!'

'Mmm... Okay, but no shop talk; the official press conference is tomorrow morning.'

'Well... maybe a little.'

'Ha. Thought so. Where and when?

'Are you in Valetta?'

'Yes.'

'Margos, one p.m. ... I have a craving for pesto sauce.'

'You're not pregnant, are you?'

'I wish.'

'Really!' It was an exclamation rather than a question.

'Oh God, I don't know. My body is telling me one thing, my head another.'

'Listen to your head, then. See you at one.'

***

Doctor Mauro Cali was slightly in awe of Duke Wayne. He himself was an exceptional doctor; he knew that, but just to be on the same team as Wayne was slightly overwhelming. Cali was from a poor background but had worked hard, studied various subjects before opting for medicine, and had practised in England, Australia and, most recently, the USA before taking up his present position in Malta a few weeks previously. He had never been so thankful about the decision to come to Malta as he was now.

'You like the movies, Mauro?' asked Duke Wayne as the two doctors sat in the hospital canteen. Mauro had never been in the canteen before, although he had been at the hospital for several months by this time. He had always liked to "maintain a certain degree of distance" from lower-level staff; but when Wayne had said 'fuck that' on hearing Cali's view, he didn't argue.

'I do, yes. As a matter of fact, I'm going to the cinema tonight.'

'Really, what are you going to see?'

'*Brokeback Mountain.*'

'Ooh, sweetie... Enjoy.' And with that, Wayne was off, leaving a crimson-faced Cali trying to ignore the titters coming from a table of nurses directly behind him.

***

Spiteri and Arrigo greeted each other with genuine affection. They were different personalities, with different views on many issues—drug use, freedom of information, to name but two—but they respected each other's positions and the views they each held. Spiteri had arrived five minutes earlier and was just finishing off a glass of wine when Arrigo came bounding through the glass doors of the pizzeria.

'I'm not late, am I?' asked Arrigo, noticing her friend's now-empty glass.

'No, no... I was early,' replied Spiteri.

The Maltese Dahlia

'Okay, let's order; I'm starving. I'm supposed to be having dinner with Nicola this evening, but half the time he cancels at the last minute, so...'

Daphne Arrigo's romance with Nicola Tizian was another one of the issues that the two friends didn't see eye to eye upon. Tizian was a wealthy entrepreneur with business interests all over the islands, but mainly in the Paceville area of St Julians, where drugs, lap dancing bars, and night clubs catered to the demands of the thousands of tourists, English language students, and Maltese youths that frequented the area. He was of Corsican extraction and, although he had been charged with no crimes on Malta, his reputation was fearsome. One story that had done the rounds a couple of years before was that if Tizian had a problem with you, then you should hope that he murders you because the alternative was worse. People were left to use their own imagination as to what that might mean. Spiteri had met him on a few occasions, some work-related, some socially; he had always been charming to her and never once said or did anything evenly remotely unacceptable. She couldn't say that she liked him, but she didn't particularly dislike him, and she accepted Daphne's decision.

The two friends ordered Fenkata, pasta with rabbit sauce, and two glasses of red wine. Arrigo had been slightly surprised by Spiteri's drink order, as she was sure the first glass had been white wine, but had more pressing things to think about. Spiteri smiled as she saw her friend taking a copy of the artist's impression of the face of the dead girl, girl 6 A and 6B, from her shoulder bag.

'You don't waste time, Daphne! *No, how are you, Thea? You're looking lovely, Thea. Is that a new hairstyle Thea; it suits you.*'

'Is it?'

'Is what it?'

'A new hairstyle?'

'No.'
'Shut up then! Right, tell all.'
'Shut up and tell all... Not sure how to do that.'
'Come on, Thea. Pretty please.'

Spiteri looked down at her glass, took a long draft, and her tone hardened. 'You can't write anything just yet, Daphne... and it's bad. The worst ever.'

'I know.'
'What, how do you know?'
'I just do. Is it true... what had been done to the girl?'
'Daphne, I don't know what you do or don't know; but like I said, it's the worst I've ever seen... or Paul Sammut, for that matter.'
'Jesus.'
'No Jesus involved in this, Daphne.'

Spiteri spent the next ten minutes relating all that she felt she could say to her friend.

'Jesus, Thea.'
'I think I've already responded to that.'
'Any thoughts, clues, anything?'
'Not really. Dr Sammut thinks maniac, Sarah thinks he'll do it again, and I always go along with poor Matt's theory: someone she knew.'

Arrigo leant over and took her friend's hand. 'It will get better in time, Thea.'

'Will it?'
'He might not do it again.'
'What, who?'
'The killer.'
'What makes you think that?'
'I want to check out a couple of things; let's meet here at the same time tomorrow, once the press conference is over.'

***

The following morning's press conference was brief and to the point. It had been agreed beforehand that only the basic details of the murder would be revealed and that only Commissioner Galea would actually speak or take questions.

Galea only took a few minutes to inform the crowded room in *Pulizija* headquarters in Floriana that the body of a female had been found in the fields near Msierah. The *Pulizija* were treating it as a murder and Inspector Thea Spiteri would be leading the investigation. 'As well as her superior officers, Inspector Spiteri will also report directly to me.' Galea then held up the artist's impression sketch and requested that if anybody recognised the person in the drawing, they should contact the *Pulizija* as soon as possible. He then intimated that he would take a few questions but that he was keen to get back to the investigation.

'Was the victim a prostitute?' someone asked.

'We have no idea at this stage who, or what, the girl was. Next.'

Daphne Arrigo stood. 'Commissioner, are you confident you will find the person responsible for this terrible crime?'

'Yes, very confident.'

'Why's that?'

'Pardon?'

'Why are you confident? The general public has no faith whatsoever in the *Pulizija*'s ability to catch anybody given your recent history.'

'That's a gross exaggeration, Ms Arrigo, and unfounded.'

'Do you feel the media has a role to play in helping you find this killer?'

'Yes, yes indeed. We always appreciate the help that the media gives us.'

'In that case, is there anything you would like to tell us about the killing; anything that might help the public to focus their minds on who the killer might be? Anything unusual, the positioning of the body... that sort of thing.'

'No. A young woman has been murdered; I would have thought that that alone would be enough to make the public think.'

'Right, so the victim wasn't cut in half, then?'

Galea looked as if he was about to explode. 'No comment.' Spiteri closed her eyes.

Arrigo persisted. 'Were body parts removed from the victim?' The room was now in a semi-uproar.

'No comment. Right, that's it. Please make sure the sketch is featured prominently in your papers.'

Spiteri entered the side room a few seconds before an enraged Galea stormed in. 'What the fuck!'

Spiteri looked the commissioner in the eye. 'Commissioner, I can assure you that Arrigo did not get that information from me. I did speak to her yesterday, but I only said that there had been a pretty gruesome killing.'

'I never thought it was you, Thea... but someone has been talking to her. Okay, get on with things and keep me up to date.'

'I will, Commissioner.' Spiteri thought it best not to mention she was going to meet Arrigo that afternoon— and that she knew exactly where Arrigo got her information.

***

Peter Abela was a happy man; a patient had just died from serious head injuries after a motor bike crash. His parents had given permission for his organs to be used. The new facility at Mater Dei would be performing its first transplant operation that night.

One issue that had always concerned Abela was the hospital's ability to get organs or limbs; and once sourced, to get them to Malta quickly enough. He had brought up the issue with Duke Wayne, but he had dismissed any concern with, 'Not a problem, Head Honcho Man. There are always ways.' Abela wasn't quite sure that he liked being addressed in that way and

The Maltese Dahlia

wouldn't accept it from anyone else, but Wayne had an aura about him that anyone would defer to. He was also a little bit annoyed that his request to be present during the transplant had been dismissed with a wave of the hand and, 'Sorry, Captain. Jabbers and pokers only in my tepee.' Abela headed for his office to make sure everything was in place for the operation in terms of the legalities and to let *The Malta Times* know about how all his hard work was coming to fruition. He called into the administration offices on the way and told one of the secretaries to call Doctor Cali and let him know about the operation going ahead.

'What if he doesn't answer?'

Abela knew that the girl was not long out of school, but silently wondered what the other interviewees were like if this one actually got the job. 'Then leave a message on his voicemail. Messages are good.'

***

Spiteri knew that Arrigo would never reveal her sources; and although she would like to know who Arrigo had spoken to, she decided to completely ignore that morning's fiasco.

Daphne Arrigo was already sitting with a coffee when Spiteri entered, a smile of satisfaction on her face.

Spiteri ordered a red wine and sat down opposite her purring friend.

'Well?' said Arrigo.

'Well what?'

'Aren't you going to grill me for my sources? Use our friendship to batter me over the head?'

'Why would I; I'm not in the slightest bit interested. We eating?'

Arrigo, slightly bemused, studied her friend's face: 'Oh, right... fair enough.'

It was Spiteri's turn to score a point, knowing anything that baffled Arrigo would torment her.

'Let me ask you something. Although the poor girl had basically been massacred, did it appear that her body was laid out in a certain way, in a provocative pose, maybe in a way to suggest she might have been a prostitute?'

'Yes.'

'It doesn't show it in this drawing, but was her face cut wide open on both sides?'

'You don't know everything, then?'

'Please, Thea. I think I can help you with this.'

'Yes, her face was cut open.'

'Have you ever heard of a famous crime in the United States; books and films have covered it to death, forgive the pun, of a murdered girl, The Black Dahlia?'

'No, I don't think so.'

'Look it up on Google when you get back to the office. Basically, everything you've described is the same as that case, almost identical. It was back in the forties or fifties. I can't remember, but it was so horrific, it's become a bit of a cult crime. The poor girl wasn't exactly a prostitute, but she seemed to have liked men, put it that way.'

'Where did the name come from?'

'Apparently she always wore black, was seen in the bars and dance halls around Hollywood every night. Someone just called her that, I suppose, and the name stuck. Come to think of it, it was probably a reporter; letting you know now, Thea... The Maltese Dahlia... I've copyright on that.'

'The Maltese Dahlia. It almost sounds like something a woman would like to be called. Was the killer executed?'

'That's the thing, Thea. The killer was never caught, and he never did it again.'

CHAPTER 3

The following morning, Spiteri read the two priority items on her desk: no matches for the fingerprints or the DNA of the murdered girl had been found. Spiteri hadn't really been surprised; she knew that this was never going to be a straightforward case. She walked out of her office into the squad room. All of her team was there, looking busy, but in reality, they did not have a lot to work on.

'Listen everyone,' said Spiteri. 'Have any of you ever heard of a famous murder from back in the nineteen-forties in America: The Black Dahlia killing?'

Michael Sammut was quick to respond. 'I'm sure I've seen a film about it. Totally crap; can't remember who was even in it.'

'Okay, all of you, onto your PCs. Google it, read up on it... I'll be testing you on it in thirty minutes.'

None of the squad was quite sure if she was serious or not; she had been acting a little bit strangely lately, a bit wandered.

***

Although she was a few years older than Michael Sammut, Sarah Said found herself quite attracted to him. He hadn't shown any interest in her, and she knew office romances were frowned upon, but she marked it down as a *possibly* in her Cranial Black Book. Said hadn't had a lot of luck in the romance stakes over the years and had been disappointed when a guy she met a few months back, and had dated a few times, decided he couldn't settle in Malta and had flown back to Australia. There had been a couple of phone calls, a couple of conversations on Skype, but it had just dwindled away. When she was dating, one of her favourite nights was cuddling up in the cinema, so that was another plus point in Sammut's score card, as he seemed to talk incessantly about films and actors and had actually timetabled a night's leave to coincide with the Oscar presentations on TV.

Her other new colleague, Dario, was also a nice guy, good looking and sharp at work, but he was married and therefore couldn't get a place in her thoughts. In fact, Grimoldi had been married twice. His first wife, who he had married when they were both nineteen, had been murdered after attending an evening class at the Mater Dei Hospital several years before. Her mutilated body had been found in some shrubbery adjacent to the hospital car park. The killer was never traced. He seemed happy with his life now though, and Said was happy for him.

The latest entry in Said's thoughts, Michael Sammut, looked up from his PC. 'My God, have you read this stuff about The Black Dahlia? Elizabeth Short, her name was... how could anyone...' He looked over at Said. 'Was that what happened to our victim?'

'Pretty much,' replied Said.

'Glad I wasn't called out, then. Dario, what do you think?'

Dario Grimoldi looked pensive. 'I'm not sure, but I'm reading here that one of the cops reckoned that it was, let me get this right, a "defiance killing"... that the brutality, the way the body was laid out, posed... was sending a message.'

The Maltese Dahlia

'Who to?' asked Sammut.

'Who knows? Some gang, the cops... God knows... They never found out.'

'Bet it was a senator, or the mayor, or the chief of police, or...'

'Joe Di Maggio?' ventured Said.

'Yea... who?' Sammut's flow was interrupted.

'Never mind. Let's solve our own killing; leave the forties to look after themselves.'

'Do you remember the case?' asked Sammut.

Said was about to have a stern word until she saw Sammut winking at Grimoldi.

'No, but I know which film icon Joe Di Maggio was married to,' replied Said as she walked out of the room.

***

'Buy body parts! Are you serious?' Peter Abela stood in the Mater Dei car park looking at Duke Wayne in a astonishment; almost spitting out his response

'Why not! I'll tell you now, it's the only way you'll build up the reputation of the unit,' replied Wayne.

'Ruin the reputation, you mean. I can't believe you're even suggesting it.'

'Hold on. Let's be clear about this. I am not "suggesting" it, merely saying that I know for a fact that it is common practice. You hold the purse strings; you are the one that has to make the business decisions.'

'Well, as far as I'm concerned, there's no decision to make.'

'Cool... but if you find yourself in a few months' time having to decide against buying a heart or closing the unit, bear this conversation in mind.' Wayne walked away, whistling some film theme tune that Abela vaguely recognised.

On his drive home, Peter Abela thought over what Wayne had said. *Just what would I do?*

***

Nicola Tizian was sitting on his usual perch in The White Line Club, going over the week's takings. He had lost track on a couple of occasions as his mind kept going back to a business proposition that had just been put to him. At first, he had thought it was a joke, a *cajta*, but when he realised that it was not and, more importantly, the sums of money involved, his attitude changed. He picked up his phone and called Daphne Arrigo. 'Darling, let's have dinner tonight.'

'Are you sure? No late call-offs?'

'I promise. There are some things I want to ask you.'

'Do they involve being naked?'

'Don't be crude, Daphne, you know I don't like it. Nine p.m. ... The Gozitan?'

'Yes, sir.'

***

Thea Spiteri sat at her desk and considered if it was possible that the killing was some sort of copy cat killing of The Black Dahlia. *Sixty years later? Surely not. But from what Daphne said, it was an iconic killing to some.* The ring of Spiteri's phone brought a stop to her musings.

'Spiteri.'

'Ma'am, it's St Julians Station. We have a woman here who says she knows the murder victim.'

'Does she seem genuine?'

'Yes, definitely.'

'Get her a coffee and put her in an interview room. I'll be there in twenty minutes.' Spiteri walked out into the squad room and looked around. 'Right, Michael, come with me.'

It took Spiteri less than fifteen minutes to reach St Julians from her office in Floriana since Sammut had obviously decided that driving like a madman would

The Maltese Dahlia

impress her. She and Sammut entered the interview room and sat down opposite a waif-like figure that looked about twelve years old; but twelve going on thirty somehow.

'Hello, I'm Inspector Spiteri. This is DC Sammut. Did you get a coffee okay?'

The girl nodded.

'So, you think you might know the girl in the drawing?'

Another nod.

'No need to be afraid, eh... what is your name?'

'Laura.'

'Okay, so Laura... who do you think the girl in the drawing might be?'

'Poppins.'

'What... Poppins... That's her name?'

'Yes.'

'Her first name?'

'Her only name. She's called that because she always carried an umbrella around, even when it wasn't raining.'

'Why did she do that?'

'She said it was to prod the balls of anyone who tried to get smart.'

Spiteri looked at the crumpled figure, desolate, slumped across from her. 'Laura, what age are you?'

'Old enough, if that's what you're thinking.' There was a certain resolve, pride even, in her tone.

'Old enough to do what, Laura?'

Laura paused, looked at the floor. 'To look after myself.'

'How do you know Poppins?'

'We worked together sometimes.'

'Doing what?'

Laura glanced up at Spiteri, said nothing.

'Laura, was Poppins a prostitute?'

'Was?'

'What?'

'You said "was"... She's dead, isn't she? She's that body you found.'

'If it is Poppins then, yes, I'm afraid so. Do you have any other names for her? Anything at all you can tell us will be a big help.'

'She told me once that she was from Sicily. She told me that she would soon have enough money to get out, go home and start a new life. She wasn't on the streets that much recently, but she had money. She didn't seem to need to work.'

'Who did she work for?'

'Same people as me. I can't say.'

'Had she been having any problems with a client recently?'

'I don't think so. Like I said, she wasn't working much. One thing strange, last time I saw her, she gave me one hundred euro and said "Nearly out girl, nearly out." She seemed very happy. She walked away down the street twirling her umbrella; she seemed happy.' Laura started to cry.

Spiteri got Sammut to take down Laura's details and drive her home. Spiteri called Arrigo.

'Daphne, can you do something for me? Can you arrange for me to have a meeting with Nic? Off the record, no snooping, I just need a bit of background information.'

'No problem. I'm meeting him tonight, as a matter of fact. I'll organise it. Can I sit-in?'

'Yes, Daphne, but you'll know what you can write and what you can't. Deal?'

'Deal. I'll get back to you.'

That evening, Arrigo told Nic about the request from Thea. 'Interesting,' replied Tizian. 'Of course, tell her three p.m. in the square at Ballutta Bay.'

'Okay. So, Mr Mysterious, what did you want to ask me?'

'What do you think of the ways I make a living, Daphne?'

The Maltese Dahlia

'I try not to.'

'Why is that? Do you disapprove?'

'I neither approve nor disapprove. What's this all about, Nicola?'

'Tell me, do you think morality should play a part in business decision-making?'

'I'd like to think so, but clearly it doesn't. Why are you asking these questions?'

'I've been made a business proposition. The nature of the business is one that I never even knew existed. The profits are huge, but there is undoubtedly a moral dilemma involved.'

'Don't do it then.'

'Okay, but if I don't do it, someone else will, so the business will still operate, so...'

'So you may as well make the money yourself?'

'Precisely.'

'What's the business?'

Nicola Tizian smiled across at Arrigo. 'Coffee?'

***

Salvatore Grasso hated his job, and he was especially unhappy about the pathetic wages he earned, but he knew he couldn't go back to prison. Even though his third child was on the way, he knew his wife, Mona, would leave him for good. Their flat in Msierah was already too small for a family of four and his wife continually let him know that she was looking for a better life than the one he was offering, and a life earned in an honest way. He was sure she still loved him, although she didn't seem overjoyed about the latest baby being on the way, and he was very much in love with her. He knew he had to find a way to bring in more money. But the only ways that Salvatore Grasso knew to bring in money could never be described as honest, and he hadn't actually been successful being dishonest, either. *This time, it is different. Desperate people will do desper-*

ate things, and these people are desperate. Or at least they will be.

Grasso's pensive mood was only broken by an overly loud tannoy announcement: "Visiting time is now over. Would all visitors now leave the hospital."

CHAPTER 4

Thea Spiteri wasn't particularly looking forward to her meeting that afternoon with Nicola Tizian. He had always treated her respectfully and, she had to admit, she had had a couple of very enjoyable nights out at gala dinners and fundraisers as Daphne Arrigo's guest, but Spiteri knew that Tizian paid the bills. Spiteri poured herself a glass of water and downed two aspirin tablets; her head felt like she had been to a gala dinner the night before instead of what she actually did, which was fall asleep on her couch after a couple of post-dinner brandies. The loud ring of her desk phone didn't help ease the pounding.

The caller's voice was very quiet, but somehow Spiteri knew straightaway who it was.

'Is that you, Laura? Are you alright?'

'Yes. You said to ring you if I knew anything that might help.'

'Yes, yes I did. What is it, Laura?'

'I know Poppins' real name now. I was talking to a... waitress... last night, and she had known Poppins from years before, although she said that Poppins hadn't recognised her. Poppins' name is, was, Letizia Corsu.'

'Thank you, Laura. That is a great help... and Laura, if you ever need my help, for anything at all, you call me, okay?'

Spiteri only heard the phone click off.

***

Mauro Cali was ecstatic. John Duke Wayne had complimented Cali's work and told him he was aware of all the hard work he was putting in and so he was taking him for lunch. He wasn't quite as pleased with the chosen venue, the Texas Steak House in Sliema, but it was the company that mattered.

'What will you have, Mauro?'

'Oh, just something light.' Cali looked up at the... *rather handsome*... young waiter and asked, 'Do you do a green salad, perhaps with French dressing, oh, and a soda and lime. Lots of ice.'

'Fuck me, Mauro. If I'd known that was your taste, I'd have just chucked you in a field and picked you up on the way back! Okay, young man, rib eye, pepper sauce, chips... oh, and you better give me some cole slaw with that before Mauro here passes out.'

The young waiter went to move off and just caught Wayne's final call. 'And a pitcher of Cisk.'

'A pitcher? Are people joining us?' asked Cali in a barely detectable despondent tone.

'No. Why are you asking that?'

'No, nothing... just wondered.'

'So Mauro, I meant to ask you but it's been hectic, as you well know. How did your movie go the other night?'

'Oh, *Brokeback Mountain*? Yes, very good, very good indeed. Have you seen it?'

'No, not my kind of movie, to be honest; more a *Scarface* type of guy.'

'Pity. The acting was wonderful, John. Heath Ledger was very alluring. Such a tragedy.'

'Why, does he get bumped off at the end?'

'Eh, no. He died... In real life, that is.'

'Pity he didn't know you, then. You might have saved him! No, joking aside Mauro, I'm very impressed by you.

The Maltese Dahlia

I know you think I'm a loud-mouthed honcho, but I know my discipline and I know who couldn't tell a heart from an ankle, and you are one of the best... and it's Duke.'

'What?'

'Duke. Call me Duke; I don't like John. Reminds me of my mother.'

'Okay, well... Duke... thank you very much for your seal of approval. Coming from you, that means a lot. You know, for a honcho.'

Wayne looked over at Cali, Cali started to go red; he wondered if he'd overstepped the mark. Suddenly, Wayne burst out laughing. 'See? I told them you had sense of humour.'

'Sorry, told who? Do people think I'm too serious? Have they been talking about me?'

'No, no... just idle chat. Anyway, let's move on. I want to ask you something. Two things, actually.'

'Fine. Please, go ahead.'

'Right, number one, what do you make of Abela?'

'Well, to be honest, I haven't really put any thought into it. He seems very efficient.'

'You think so? Good, because that leads to question two. Do you have good contacts, people to ease the path?'

'Sorry, J... Duke. I don't quite understand.'

'Limbs, organs... Do you have a supply source?'

Cali was taken aback. 'A supply source? What do you mean? The hospitals find suitable organs and bring them in, I've never...'

'Yea? Well answer me this. Do you think Abela has got what it takes to get us everything we need?'

'He's invested a lot in the department.'

John Duke Wayne leaned across the table 'I'm talking about parts, partner, fucking body parts. What do you think will happen to our, our, department if Abela can't cut it? Our reputations in tatters, that's what. We'd be known as the two guys who were handed the Golden

Egg... and ended up dropping it. Do you think that a fucking accountant will be able to compete with the real players in getting his way?'

'The real players?'

'Oh, come on, Mauro. You can't have been in this game as long as you have without knowing what's what.'

'It seems that I have... and I don't.'

'Business, Mauro. Supply and demand. The person who gets things is the person who walks over the other guy to get it.'

'Well...'

'Well nothing, Mauro. I meant what I said: you're the best. I want you as my right-hand man... but my right-hand man in everything. If you can't give me that, then walk away. I'll give you a great reference, but I am staying here and putting Mater Dei on the map. So... yes or no, Mauro?'

Cali was still unsure what exactly he was being asked, but he knew he wasn't walking away from working with Duke Wayne; he leaned over the table and stretched out his hand. 'Howdy, Sheriff. Meet your new Deputy. Let's do what needs to be done.'

Wayne roared with laughter. 'I told them. I fucking told them.'

***

Nicola Tizian was already seated and had ordered a bottle of mineral water and a cappuccino. He stood up when Arrigo and Spiteri approached, kissed Arrigo, nodded at Spiteri, and indicated for the women to sit. He ordered two further cappuccinos before turning his attention to Spiteri.

'So, Inspector, how can I help you?'

'You'll no doubt be aware from the papers—and Daphne, no doubt—about the dismembered body that has been found.'

'Yes. Dreadful, absolutely dreadful. Have you identified the girl yet?'

'Well, that is why I'm here, actually. The girl is Sicilian apparently, was working in Malta as a prostitute.'

Tizian's eyes narrowed slightly but never wavered from Spiteri's. 'And so you linked her to me?'

'Not linked, no, but I thought you might give me some background information that might prove useful.'

Tizian paused for a moment. 'And trip myself up possibly?'

Spiteri never replied.

'Inspector, I know that you neither like nor approve of me.' He raised his hand to stop Spiteri from interrupting. 'That is your prerogative. Daphne tells me you are a good and fair person, non-judgemental. That is good enough for me, but if I find out that you are using our association in this to try and undermine my business, then all deals are off. Do you agree?'

'Yes.'

'Good. What would you like to know?'

'Thank you. Let's agree about the basics, Nicola. We know that Sicilian Mafia families are heavily involved in prostitution here on Malta. What I don't know is are these people prepared to go to these lengths over some prostitution issue?'

Tizian smiled. 'Inspector, how would I know? I am Corsican. Corsicans are not Italian. They are French, or of French extraction, at least. Yes, many Italians have settled in Corsica, and vice versa, but the country still considers itself French, and that is the language they speak, not Italian.'

'And you, can you speak French?'

'*Mais oui*, and Italian and English, but not Maltese... a barbaric language!'

'Watch it,' cried Arrigo. Everyone laughed, and the tension eased.

'Inspector, all I can do is to give you a little background on the little I know about Sicilians. In more recent times, since the war, say, the Corsican Mafia has become very involved in the international drug trade. It was well known that they had a huge network, even stretching to the USA, for distributing cigarettes. Eventually, they were approached by the Sicilian Mafia to start using these routes for drugs. Not all on the Corsican side wanted to do it; an internal war for control took place. Those in favour of getting involved in drugs won. The Brise de Mer gang controlled Northern Corsica and the Colonna clan the South. But, as is the way with these things, internal fighting and greed took over, culminating in what became known as The French Connection. You may have seen the film. Gene Hackman was in it, very good... surprisingly accurate. Anyway, that basically killed off the two gangs. The two in charge now are the Venzolasca gang, who took over from Brise de Mer, and The Petit Bar Gang. There are lots of family groups, et cetera, in both gangs, for example, the Valincos and the Marseille group.'

'The Marseille group. So the French Connection is still alive and well?' asked Spiteri.

Tizian shrugged. 'I wouldn't know.'

'Nicola, please don't be offended, but the girl's body was terribly mutilated. Would you say that that kind of thing is, not accepted or commonplace as such, but in some way accepted in Mafia circles because of some sort of code or as retribution for a certain kind of betrayal, perhaps?'

'How did she actually die?'

'Blows to the head.'

'Daphne tells me the poor girl was tortured?'

'Yes.'

'Then my view would be that it was done either by some crazed madman or someone with a grievance, real or perceived: a client, boyfriend... if it were Sicilian Mafia, she would have been shot and the body buried. I will ask around and get back to you.'

'Did you know her, Nicola?'

The Maltese Dahlia

Tizian's eyes again narrowed, but this time a wry grin accompanied it. 'How can I tell? you never told me her name.'

It was Spiteri's turn to display a wry grin.

***

Commissioner of *Pulizija* Kevin Galea sat at his desk, his mind racing between different issues: one being what comes first, your family or your duty and, secondly, what to do when there is a conflict in your life involving your duty, your morality, and your own family. He felt sorry to bring Thea Spiteri into the issue but he had to have absolute faith in anyone he confided in over his dilemma. He picked up the phone and called Spiteri.

'Thea, can you come and see me, tomorrow morning at ten a.m.?'

'Of course I'll be there,' replied Spiteri.

'Any progress with the Dahlia killing? That is not what tomorrow is about, incidentally.'

'I wouldn't exactly say progress, Commissioner. We have her name and we know she was working as a prostitute. She was from Sicily originally... I met up with Nicola Tizian this morning. He's offered to help.'

'Tread very carefully there, Thea.'

'I know, but I feel it's worth a try.'

'Okay. See you tomorrow.'

***

I am so happy. Everything has fallen into place. My calling is clear now. I have been shown the path. I will begin my work. I will start my preparations on Friday; on Saturday, it will begin. What should I wear? Should I go early or late? Late... darker. This will bring me so much prestige. I will be famous at last.

CHAPTER 5

Thea Spiteri sat down opposite Commissioner Galea and could see the strain in his eyes. Spiteri had gotten to know the commissioner well over the last difficult year; she trusted him but did worry that the strain of the post might be too much for him. His predecessor had been a political animal, a dealmaker. Galea was a policeman first.

'Thea, I know you have a lot on with this Dahlia case, but I consider you to be my best investigator, and the most discrete, so I want you to quietly look into something for me. Do what you want and talk to whoever you want, but no other officer is to know what you're doing—at this stage, anyway.'

'And what am I doing?'

'My daughter, Josephine—Jo-Jo we call her—is very ill, terminally in fact... unless she gets a new heart.'

'God, Kevin. I'm sorry to hear that.'

'This sort of thing is a waiting game, as you probably know. It's terrible; you're basically sitting, hoping someone will die so you can use their organs. We've been told by the hospital, Mater Dei obviously, that they're doing all they can, but...' Galea looked away, took a deep breath. 'Then, two nights ago, my wife gets a phone call. The caller says that he is very sorry to hear about our predicament and that he thinks he can help... for twenty thousand euro.'

'What, he will supply a heart? How does he know it would be a match? Where is the heart coming from?'

'He explained that the concept of perfect matches is a fallacy. As long as certain criteria are met, then the operation can go ahead. He also made the point that Jo Jo would die anyway and that surely we should try everything. After that, the body will either accept or reject the heart, so-called perfect match or not. He said that he makes no apology for what he does, that rightly or wrongly, body parts were a business, and like all business, it was governed by supply and demand. She was stunned, was just sitting, staring into space when I got home. She told me what had happened and that the man was going to call again tonight for our answer.'

Spiteri hesitated momentarily. 'And what is your answer, Kevin?'

'My wife wants us to pay.'

'Your daughter's married, isn't she? What does her husband think?'

'Yes, to Salvatore Grech. Jo Jo adores him, calls him Torri for short. You know, her tower. My wife is not so infatuated; he's always coming up with grand business schemes but nothing ever seems to come to fruition. I think he's harmless enough, and as I said, my daughter dotes on him and so I do my best to keep the peace. Anyway, the truth is, Thea, we haven't told him. He wouldn't see an issue. Insist on paying.'

'Forgive me, but do you have that kind of money?'

'Between us, yes.'

'What do you want to do? Incidentally, this conversation hasn't taken place.'

'It's illegal, Thea... I can't do it.'

'Is it? Is it actually against the law? For him, yes, but if he had, as he seems to have, some way of supplying the hospital with the heart, is it a crime for you to use it? I don't think so.'

'Thank you, Thea. I know you are trying to help me, but I would be complicit, you must see that. What would you do?'

'I don't have any family as such, but if I could have bought an illegal body part to save Matt's life back at the time, I would have done it. No question. Sorry.'

Galea nodded. 'Thank you for your honesty, Thea. Everyone must do what they think is right. This is what I want you to do. Find out if there is any evidence of a paid-for body parts trade going on, in general terms, and then if it is happening at Mater Dei. This whole thing could just be an attempted scam on us. When this guy phones back, I'll tell him yes, find out as much as I can, pass it on to you.'

Spiteri left Galea's office in a bit of a daze. She felt so sorry for him, for the moral dilemma that was obviously torturing him. She decided to have an off-the-record chat with Paul Sammut.

***

The Chief Exec of Mater Dei Hospital, Peter Abela, loved Gozo, especially the area around his home village of Gharb. His parents still lived in the razzett where he was born and grew up, and so he tried to get over to Malta's sister island as often as his work schedule allowed. He especially liked to visit when he was troubled, like he was now. Abela liked nothing better than to stroll along the dusty paths that meandered through the fields of oranges and lemons, St Dimitri Church on the left, the Lighthouse at Gordan on the right, and end up looking out on the azure sea from the cliffs at Hekka Point. Today, though, he had reached the cliffs without really taking in any of the scenery. His dream, the one he had turned into reality, the transplant department at Mater Dei, would soon be in financial trouble. The availability of organs and limbs, and the trouble of getting suitable ones to Malta in good condition, was proving more difficult than he had expected. Duke Wayne did not seem concerned, but as Abela had rather irritably said to him yesterday, 'Yes, well Duke, you only have to spend the money. I have to bring it in.' Wayne had simply turned and walked away, whistling the tune to *The Magnificent Seven*.

***

DS Dario Grimoldi loved his second wife. There was no doubt about that in his mind. She looked after the house—and him. She also looked after her aged mother's house, made her breakfast and dinner, and put her to bed at night. She dressed demurely and had no disgusting desires in the bedroom. She was everything a wife should be, unlike his first wife. It had only been a matter of weeks after getting married to his first wife that he had realised she was a whore. Not a whore who sold her body, but a whore nevertheless. Low-cut tops, short dresses, bikini on the beach, not a swimsuit. Grimoldi did love her, obsessed over her, knew that accepting her ways was the only way that he could keep her. He had tried to change her, pointed out that she didn't need to show her beauty to other men, that it would only lead to trouble. He had suggested they start a family, but she had only laughed and said she wanted a career, a life, before she became a "fat little Maltese wife who sat on the pavement talking to all the other fat little Maltese wives."

Grimoldi was sitting at his desk in the squad room, looking at photos of the Dahlia killing, remembering his friend and colleague, Gino, coming to his door, his eyes red with tears. He remembered that they never spoke in the squad car on the way to the hospital car park. He remembered looking down at his wife's violated body. Her skirt at her ankles, her red V-neck top ripped and torn, her red bra pulled down around her navel... and the blood... he remembered the blood... everywhere. He also remembered that he felt nothing.

***

Unusually, when Thea Spiteri had called Paul Sammut, he had answered his phone himself.

'Don't tell me you have nothing gruesome to do today, Paul?' asked Spiteri.

'I know. It's awful; I'm at a loss, myself. I have a mountain of paperwork obviously—when do I not?—people can be more trouble when they are dead than when they're alive!'

'Well, your problem is solved; I am taking you to lunch.'

'It's not Michael, is it?'

'What... No. Nothing like that.'

They arranged to meet in a half hour at the Pasha restaurant in San Gwan, both arriving within minutes of each other. They ordered Timpana for Sammut, Ravjul for Spiteri. On her way to the restaurant, Spiteri had accepted that, if there was anything sinister going on at Mater Dei, Sammut could conceivably be involved, but had decided it was so unlikely that she was worrying about nothing.

They chatted aimlessly whilst waiting for the food to arrive and sipped at the wine they had ordered. The food arrived and the waiter disappeared into the kitchen

'So, Thea, to what do I owe the pleasure?'

'Paul, there is a very delicate matter I need to discuss with you. I know that under normal circumstances, I wouldn't have to say to you about confidentiality, but these are no ordinary circumstances. I'm hoping that they are no circumstances at all, but it is an investigation.'

Sammut nodded. 'Of course. Go on; I'm intrigued.' Paul Sammut silently noted that Spiteri had not said "official investigation."

Spiteri told Sammut of the issue, leaving out Commissioner Galea's involvement.

'Good God, incredible. Do you believe it?'

'I have an open mind. I must have; it's my job. '

Sammut hesitated, then said, 'What is your source? Is he reliable?'

'I can't say, but yes,' replied Spiteri.

'I have heard that the new department is not as busy, or efficient, as they had hoped... but these things do take a long time.'

'Tell me, Paul. Is there such a thing as an organ trade?'

'Oh yes, definitely... A big business, unfortunately.'

'Have you ever been approached?'

'No.'

'Okay. You understand I had to ask, Paul. Take it as a compliment; I could only ask someone I trusted.' Spiteri leaned over and squeezed Sammut's hand.

'How is Michael doing, Thea?'

'Well, he's only been with me a short time, as you know, but, yes, he's fine.'

'Right.' Sammut's demeanour alerted Spiteri.

'What is it?'

'Oh, and don't take this the wrong way please, Thea, but Michael's mother and I had high hopes for Michael. He could have been a doctor, you know, even a surgeon; who knows? But he was bloody obsessed with being an actor, wasted years prancing around, spent whole weekends watching films and plays. Don't get me wrong, Thea: if the boy is happy, then that is all that matters... we're maybe just interfering parents!'

'It's okay, Paul. I understand. I wish I had had parents worrying about me.'

'Yes, I know your history. You have done well, Thea.' Sammut looked at his watch. 'I have to go now, Thea. Are you coming?'

'No, I've a couple of calls to make; may as well do them from here.'

'Okay, and thanks for lunch.'

Spiteri watched as Sammut crossed the road and got into his car. She called the waiter over and ordered a double brandy. She never made any calls.

CHAPTER 6

Despite feeling drowsy and nauseous, Thea Spiteri strode confidently into her office the following morning at seven-thirty a.m. When she saw that none of her team had arrived yet, she dropped her bag on the floor, put two aspirins in the bottom of her coffee mug, added two heaped spoonfuls of coffee, poured in some boiling water, and back-heeled her office door closed before slumping on her desk.

After what seemed like only a few seconds but was in fact fifteen minutes, Spiteri was startled to life by the ring of her desk phone.

'Spiteri.'

'He called.' Spiteri didn't need to ask who the caller was, or who he was referring to. Spiteri thought she could detect a quiver in Galea's voice, but he was still definitely in control.

'What did you do?'

'I agreed, but Thea, I want to conduct this thing as a sting operation. I want the bastard caught.'

'If he is genuine, can really get a heart, what will you do?'

'Arrest him.'

'I spoke in confidence to Paul Sammut. He confirmed that the organs business is a reality, alright but that he had never been approached and he had never heard so much as a whisper of any such goings-on at Mater Dei.'

'Was that wise? He could be involved.'

'Commissioner, I had to start somewhere and if Paul Sammut is involved then we are all doomed. We can all just pack up and go home.'

'You're right, Thea. As I said, you are my best officer; do what you feel you have to do.'

'Commissioner, at least one person at Mater Dei must be involved in this; it just couldn't be done otherwise. Can you use your contacts to get a list of the hospital's personnel; I think it would be better going through you rather than an individual officer, I'm sure you can think of some "politically correct" or "statistical" reason.'

'Ha, I'll say it's to do with an "overfunding investigation involving political corruption"... They'll be the ones needing a heart transplant after that.'

Spiteri admired the man's courage but sensed his despair; she hesitated, then asked, 'How is your daughter, Kevin?'

'No change, but that is good.'

'Good. Let me know when you have the names.'

'I will.'

***

The road between Marsaskala and Haz-Zabbar can be very busy, with locals and tourists alike heading to and from the seaside village famous for its fish restaurants. Piere Arnaud, the head of the electricity organisation Enemalta, and his wife, Maddie, were grateful that on this occasion, the road was quiet. They would be able to get to their favourite eatery, enjoy their Pixxispad cutlets, and get home before the five p.m. rush.

For a split second, the couple both thought that the blinding flash was just the sun's rays on their windscreen. Then the searing heat and strange, accelerated sideways movement puzzled them; then they were dead. Piere Arnaud's head was found some one hundred metres from the burnt-out shell that was once his pride and joy BMW. Maddie Arnaud appeared to be sleeping, sitting up and propped against the base of a eucalyptus tree. It wasn't until a motorist who had stopped behind the carnage ran over to her that he could see that she wasn't actually against the tree. It was possible that her body, propelled out of the car by the explosion of the car bomb beneath her husband's seat, could have survived if it hadn't been impaled on a long-ago abandoned and rusted scythe.

Twenty minutes later, Duty Magistrate Zammit, Commissioner Galea, Deputy Commissioner Valletta, members of the bomb disposal team, a police dog team, and several police personnel were at the scene.

'Well, what do you think, Kevin?' asked Zammit.

'Definitely a bomb,' replied Commissioner Galea.

'Yes, but do you think it's connected to our investigation?'

'It's hard to say. Yes, that would be your first reaction, but it seems a bit drastic, don't you think? These guys were amateurs, after all, if we're being honest. Maybe Arnaud was involved in things we know nothing about.'

Spiteri, Said, and Grimoldi stood surveying the scene of devastation.

'Shit, somebody wanted him dead for sure,' said Grimoldi.

Spiteri told her colleagues what she wanted. 'There is a possible starting point. I want you both to look into the ongoing investigation surrounding Enemalta. Don't dwell on the bottom rungs; see if you can find any links to something, somebody, higher up the food chain. Report everything back to me.'

She left the scene after a short conversation with Galea. Said went to talk to the bomb people to try to establish how sophisticated the bomb was.

Grimoldi walked over to Maddie Arnaud's body. She was obviously a lady who had liked to pamper herself. Immaculate hair, slightly tousled by the blast, and surprisingly neat, manicured nails, subtle make-up, expensive—but now ripped and blood-stained—clothes. Grimoldi hunkered down, whispered, 'Well, lady, where has all this titillation got you? At least the undertaker won't have to do much for you.' Grimoldi detected rather than heard a footstep behind him. He looked over his shoulder. Said was standing a few feet away.

'That's nice, Dario.'

Grimoldi was uncertain what to do. 'What is?'

'Saying a prayer for her; everyone needs a prayer.'

'Yes... Thanks.'

***

Michael Sammut was bored and frustrated. Every other officer seemed to be out at crime scenes or investigating current cases; he was compiling a table of break-in statistics involving illegal immigrants. He clicked onto the Internet and checked what was on in the cinema that weekend.

'Oh yes... thank you, God. Tomorrow night, I'll be there, astrology man!'

***

The following morning had gone pretty much along the same lines as every morning that week for Thea Spiteri: first into the office, black coffee, two aspirin, head on desk. This time, it was her mobile that rang. She picked it up, squinted her eyes to see who was calling her this early: Daphne.

'Hi.'

'You okay? You sound... well, ill,' said Arrigo.

'I'm fine. A bit tired, that's all.'

'I've got to see you... It's mega.'

The Maltese Dahlia

'Okay. When?'

'Now, woman... No time like the present... I'm in Guy's Bar across the square. I'll give you five minutes.'

'How do you know I'm in the office?'

'I waited for you going in, gave you five minutes to get a coffee, or that piss water in there you call coffee, then rang. Get over here, girl... Real coffee and a real scoop!'

Ten minutes later, Spiteri arrived in Guy's. Arrigo was a good reader of people and she suspected that all was not well with her friend, and she felt she knew why.

'Is everything okay, Thea?'

'I told you I'm just tired.'

The two women looked each other in the eye. 'If you say so, Thea... but I'm always here if you need to talk.'

'Well, that's what we're here for, so talk.'

'A massive story is about to break.'

'Oh yes, pray tell.' Spiteri knew that Arrigo was the best in the business, but sometimes even she got it wrong; the classic being when she traced Lord Lucan to a remote razzett in Mizieb.

'That new department in Mater Dei, the transplant wing. Rumours of dodgy dealings.'

Spiteri almost spat out her coffee. 'What kind of rumours?'

Arrigo studied her friend. 'My God.'

'What?'

'You know about this.'

'About what, exactly?'

'Selling parts and limbs.'

'Who is?'

'I don't know.'

'Who told you, then?'

Arrigo grimaced at her friend and ignored the question.

'So what is it you've heard, Thea? We can compare notes.'

This time, it was Spiteri's turn to ignore her friend.

'Nothing. I've got to go. Women cut in half and couples getting blown up in cars wait for no man... or woman.'

'Oh that, the car bomb? It should take you all of ten minutes to solve that.'

'Really, how's that?'

'Well, it's obvious who was behind it.'

'Not to me.'

'Debono.'

This time, Spiteri did actually choke on her coffee.

'Debono! Former Commissioner of Police, Ix-Xih, now leading politician Debono? You're mad.'

'Really? Why do you think the guy was killed, Thea? He sent someone an excessive electricity bill?"

'I've no idea. Enlighten me.'

'He was going to name names in that upcoming enquiry... so... bang.'

'"So... bang"... I don't need to ask where you're getting your information, Daphne.'

'Doesn't make it wrong, Thea. Right, one good turn and all that.'

'You're right.'

'About Mater Dei?'

'Yes.' Spiteri rose and headed for the door.

'Wait... Give me something, Thea.'

Spiteri glanced around the coffee shop; there were no other customers. 'Okay... They've been caught transplanting the legs from dead tall people onto dwarfs.'

'What!'

'Sorry, but that's the long and the short of it. Bye.'

'I'll remember this, Inspector!' Arrigo only just managed to get her words out through her laughter.

***

Duke Wayne's downtime in Malta had not been wasted. He knew, being American, that if you wanted the big bucks then you cultivated politicians, especially ones with access to funding. A little bit of research was done and Wayne had soon come up with the name Debono. The fact that Debono was ex-*Pulizija* was a concern at first, but Wayne balanced that with the fact that if anything was being looked at by the *Pulizija*, Debono would be tipped off. He had also found out that Debono had left the *Pulizija* under a bit of a cloud, which was even better. At first, Wayne had considered bringing Abela in on his strategy of wooing politicians but decided against it on the grounds that he considered Abela to be "a filly in a field of mustangs." Wayne had subsequently called Debono and a meeting had been arranged.

***

Mauro Cali neither knew of, nor cared about, the nuances of political intrigue, so never wasted time thinking about it. He also knew that he wasn't gay.

It was true that he did not find women sexually attractive, but he did not find men attractive, either. He had spent time in the past trying to work out why this would be, this characteristic that seemed to set him apart from other people. What Cali did find attractive was expertise and power. Someone who had the charisma to go out and capture the world; John Duke Wayne was such a man in Cali's eyes.

Cali opened his desk drawer and took out the cinema ticket he had bought that afternoon for the first evening show that night. 'A night with the stars in more ways than one, Mauro.'

***

A few corridors away from where Cali was sitting pondering his life, Paul Sammut was on a call.

'Yes, I'm sure I could arrange that,' he said.

'When?' said the caller.

'Well, who knows for sure? Possibly when the next suitable body comes in.'
'Suitable body?'
'Well you want it to match your requirements.'
'Yes, okay.'
'Okay... I'll call you and let you know.'

***

Although it was after six p.m. and all her team had left for the night, Thea Spiteri was still sitting at her desk. Despite more than a week having past, The Maltese Dahlia case was going nowhere, and the rumour about Debono actually scared her. She mentally checked if she had wine at home, or if she would need to buy some on the way there. She crossed over to her office door, switched off the lights, and headed out into the gloom of her nights.

CHAPTER 7

Spiteri had given her squad the weekend off, but she herself had decided to split her weekend into two: Saturday—The Dahlia case; Sunday—trying to establish if there was any truth in the body parts rumour at Mater Dei. Each day had been equally successful; she'd gotten nowhere with either case. The murder of Letizia Corsu, The Maltese Dahlia, had gone completely cold, and Spiteri could find nothing linking any of the Mater Dei staff to the transplants department, to anything remotely suspicious, nevermind criminal.

By four p.m. on Sunday afternoon, even Spiteri had had enough and so decided to pack up and go. *Go where, Thea? Home? There's no one there. For a meal? Who with? You have one friend, and she's in love with a gangster. Visit your parents? That would be nice if I only knew who they were.*

She walked over to the bookcase that stood beside the window of her office. She pushed aside her copies of *Pulizija* Annual Reports for 2002 and 2004 and took out the bottle of Hennessey brandy she kept there for emergencies. She looked down at a small Floriana park that sat between *Pulizija* headquarters and the busy bus station in Valletta. One or two young couples were walking hand in hand through the park; some older couples sat on benches, possibly watching the young lovers... and remembering. At her desk Spiteri, poured a glass of brandy. walked over and switched her office lights off, then sat on the windowsill; observing a life she would never have. She watched the young couples; did her mother and father ever walk hand in hand? Were they in love? What drove her mother to abandon her? Did she, or her father, ever think of her? Were they even alive? Spiteri sipped her drink. Her throat burned momentarily, then she felt the warm glow she had come to depend on. She glanced back at the older couples. They hardly spoke to each other, but they were content-looking. She had envisaged that contentment for her and Matt, maybe even one day to be sitting watching their own children. Spiteri rose quickly, gulped down the remains of her brandy, and walked out of her office. She didn't notice the light on her voicemail flashing.

***

Whilst Thea Spiteri had spent her Saturday morning working, Peter Abela had driven up to Gozo to visit his parents and was sitting in their front room, a former stable, on the Sunday evening when he got the call saying that the spare organs and fibula that they had been trying to source had been delivered by courier to the front desk at Mater Dei. Abela was unsure just how that had come about, as usually there was prior notice of a delivery and quite a bit of red tape to wade through; but it being a Sunday in Malta had maybe had something to do with it, and if he was honest, he didn't really care; three more operations could now go ahead. He was a happy man.

***

Dario Grimoldi loved spending time with his family. He had spent the weekend on Gozo with them, and while they liked to play at the beach at Ramla Bay, he preferred to wander around and get some exercise at the same time. He had walked up the steep slope to the cave where, legend has it, that the siren Calypso had lived and enticed ships to their destruction on the rocks with her haunting songs. The cave itself was now cordoned off because of subsidence, but the views down onto the bay, and North as far as Gordan lighthouse, were worth the effort.

Grimoldi sat at a bench across from the orchards surrounding the cave's entrance and watched as young girls, tourists and Maltese, wandered around with so few clothes on, they may as well have been naked. He watched as the men in the snack bars ogled the girls—not in admiration, but with lust. He didn't care too much about the tourists, the Scandinavians being the worst, but he felt like grabbing the Maltese girls and asking them how they expected to attract a good man when they walked around like whores. His anger was growing so much at the girls' obvious flirting with the local boys that he strode off towards the resort of Marsalforn, deciding he would get a beer there and then rejoin his family on Ramla beach.

***

At approximately the same time as Peter Abela was receiving his welcome call from the hospital, Michael Sammut was far from happy at the conversation he was having. He had just had yet another argument with his parents. He realised if he wanted to live his life the way he wanted, and indulge in his own passions, he would need to get his own flat. Yes, his mother was the one who did the washing and yes, his top and trousers were a real mess, being covered in oil, caked in dust and what appeared to be blood, but if she didn't want to wash them, then throw them out. Stop talking to him as if he was ten years old.

'What were you even doing on Gozo, and where did the blood come from? That's what I want to know,' his mother had yelled.

'I told you, a few of us went up to the festival weekend in Il-Qala; you know what it's like. Well, if you can ever remember being young, that is,' Michael had replied.

'Yes, but you're not young, Michael, and you're a policeman; although why that is, I'll never know.'

His father had sat in the corner, reading the Sunday papers, and never got involved. Michael had noticed that his father had become very distant from him since their last encounter, when he had told his father just how he felt about the way he obviously viewed his son. He realised he had hurt his father, and he did regret that, but his father's stoic response wasn't helping the situation.

***

Duke Wayne had been surprised when he walked into the foyer of the Hilton hotel in St Julians. Minister Debono was sitting with another man; Wayne had assumed it would just be the two of them, and said so as Debono rose and shook hands.

'Don't worry. He is the soul of discretion and is one of the most prominent businessmen on the island. Let me introduce you. Doctor Wayne, this is Nicola Tizian.'

***

I have never been so happy. Friday night showed me how everything fits into place. She was picked out to be the first, but she won't be the last. All it needs is to be shown who was to be chosen, and proper planning. I understand everything now. That rush between my legs last night, that explosion of emotion I have never felt before, a throbbing I must feel again.

CHAPTER 8

As usual, Thea Spiteri was first into the office on the Monday morning, but Grimoldi, Said, and Sammut were all only five minutes behind her. Spiteri waited till they all had had time to get a coffee and then called them into her office.

'Morning. I hope you all had a good weekend. I have to say that there doesn't seem to be much progress with the two main cases we're working on. I'm not criticising; I spent the weekend looking over what I could and came up with nothing new myself. So, unless something new comes to light on The Maltese Dahlia—God, how terrible, we all just seem to call her that now, poor girl.'

'Not so poor,' interrupted Sammut.

'What?' said Spiteri.

'A fair amount of money in her bank account, or should I say, accounts.'

'How much?'

'In total, more than twenty thousand euro.'

'Well, well. Why isn't this information in the system?'

'I only got confirmation from Banif about five p.m. on Friday... They are so slow. I'll put it on now.'

'Okay, and then I want you to join forces with Sarah and Dario.'

Sammut was inwardly delighted: *At last.*

'Listen, what I am about to tell you is pure rumour. Even so, not a word leaves this team. Understand?'

All three responded, 'Yes.'

'Right, it has been suggested that there is a link between the car bombing last week and former Commissioner Debono, now MP Debono.'

'Christ.'

'Indeed, but, as I said, it is a rumour. What I want the three of you to work on is to try and establish any sort of link between the dead man, Arnaud, and Debono. In fact, include Arnaud's wife in that, too. She was a socialite apparently.'

'Definitely. You could tell just by looking at her,' said Grimoldi.

'Sorry?' responded Spiteri.

'Well, I'm sorry, Ma'am, but you could tell from the way she was dressed, made up... you know.'

'No, I don't know. Dario, stay on after Sarah and Michael leave. Okay, any questions? You're clear about what I want you to do?'

'Yes,' said Sammut.

'Do you have an idea what the link might be?' asked Said.

'Not really, but Arnaud was about to be a witness in a big trial, I'd start there... but forget about the case as such; I'm only interested in any Debono link. Got that?'

Said and Sammut nodded and left.

'That was a ridiculous and, to be honest, worrying statement you just came out with, Sergeant.'

'Sorry.'

'Never mind sorry; is that really how your mind works? If it is, you're off my team, and I mean now.'

'No, no... It just didn't come out right. All I meant was that yes, she did look like a socialite.'

Spiteri studied Grimoldi's face. 'I'll let it pass this time, but one more sweeping generalisation like that, especially in a murder case, and you're on constant night patrol in Paceville. On you go... and ask Sammut to bring me a coffee please.'

A few minutes later, Sammut entered Spiteri's office with her coffee.

'Thank you, Michael. I'm sorry; I don't usually ask people to bring me coffee, but truth is I have a blinding headache.'

'No problem. Can I get you anything else?'

'No, it's fine. Michael, take a seat. We can take this opportunity to have a chat.'

'Has my father been speaking to you?'

Spiteri was slightly taken aback. 'No, why are you asking that?'

'Well, I know you and he are kind of friends... and, well, he's not exactly over the moon about me being a policeman.'

'What about you?'

'What about me?'

'Are you over the moon about it?'

Sammut paused for a few moments. 'It's my chosen career. "Over the moon." That's a difficult thing to quantify, but I am happy, if that counts.'

'It counts for quite a lot, I'd say. So, what did you do with your free weekend?'

Sammut looked at Spiteri, a slight smile on his face. 'Are you sure you haven't been speaking to my father?'

'Yes... I'm sure.'

'I went to the cinema on Friday night, then had a bit of a wild weekend on Gozo. So I'm in the bad books at home. I should get my own place, really.'

'A wild weekend on Gozo! Bit of a contradiction in terms there, Detective Constable.'

'Not if you know where to go, Ma'am.'

'I won't ask. Okay, on you go, detect something for me.'

Spiteri noticed her voicemail light flashing.

As he got up, Sammut accidently brushed against a pile of files on Spiteri's desk, sending them cascading onto the floor. Sammut muttered an apology and got down on his knees to collect up the files. Spiteri pressed the red flashing light on her desk phone that indicated she had messages.

This is your messaging service. You have 2 Messages.
Message 1. "Jake Gyllenhall."
Message 2. "Have you checked his stars, Inspector?"

Sammut got up from the floor and looked at Spiteri. She shrugged: 'No idea. I get obscure messages from time to time. There are some rather sad individuals about.'

'Do you know who Jake Gyllenhall is, Ma'am?'
'No.'
'He's an actor. Been in a lot of good movies.'
'Okay, but I'm not sure I'm any the wiser.'
'Can you play the second message again... please?'
Spiteri played the message and then looked at Sammut, eyebrows raised. 'Well?'
'Sorry... no idea.'

***

Although it was nine a.m. on a Monday morning and there were spots of rain in the air, three men strode into Mater Dei Hospital, each enthralled by their own achievements. The organ and limb supply chain that Peter Abela had organised was obviously now working well, Duke Wayne had moved one step closer to his own dream, and Mauro Cali had arranged a date: *Yes, Mauro, an all singing and all dancing bona fide date!*

Cali wasn't quite sure how he had managed it, and he had been so nervous about it that, as he made a belated attempt to empty some boxes and cases still full from his move to Malta, he had dropped a folder containing all his certificates and private papers. He bent down and started reminiscing about the hard road he had travelled to get to where he was now: pictures of his mother, drawings and certificates from school and college. His degree in Computer Science, his qualification as a yachtsman, his PADI Deep Water Instructor Certificate and, pride of place, his Doctor of Medicine certificate: *Not bad for a boy from nothing. Well, I am an important man now.*

CHAPTER 9

Thea Spiteri wasn't long out of the shower when she heard her mobile ring. She looked at the screen and saw Commissioner Galea's name.

'Hello, Commissioner.'

'Thea, I'm sorry to call you so early, but there has been a development. We got a call from Mater Dei about an hour ago to say that the operation on Jo Jo is scheduled for one p.m.'

Spiteri paused momentarily. 'Kevin, I'm glad... Some things are more important than others.'

'That's just it, Thea. There hasn't been another call from the extortionist. No one has asked for money.'

'Maybe he'll call later.'

'Maybe, but once the operation is done, what leverage would he have?'

Spiteri was silent, deep in thought.

'Okay, I need to go; I just wanted to let you know,' said Galea.

'Okay... Good luck.'

***

Nicola Tizian sat having breakfast, deep in thought over the proposal that had been outlined at the Sunday night meeting with Debono and Wayne. Although he had

had many dealings with Debono in the past—indeed, had been close friends—he didn't like him now... as a man. No honour; making money for himself was his only driver. Debono had been worth cultivating when he rose to *Pulizija* Commissioner, but politicians in Malta were ten a penny. Added to that, he had decided almost immediately that he did not like this John Duke Wayne character either; brash Americans had never been to his taste. He had had the chance to move to America many times, but the notion had never appealed. No, he would go with the person who had already approached him with a similar proposition; a proposition he had frowned upon at first, but now realised could be very lucrative. He saw that there could still be potential benefits in including Debono, if only for the influence he could exert on fellow politicians, but he had already spent a considerable of time putting plans in place to get Debono out of the way , and he wasn't changing his plans now. The arrogant American was definitely out. Had Tizian known that after he left the Hilton, Wayne had leaned over and asked Debono if Tizian had known John Gotti, he might well have put him out of the way permanently.

***

Galea's early morning call had held Spiteri up so that by the time she got into the office, her officers were already there.

Michael Sammut had started pouring over Arnaud's bank accounts to try and spot a link to Debono, but only after looking up Jake Gyllenhall's star sign. The actor had been born on 19th December 1980, and so was a Sagittarius. Sammut mulled this over for ten minutes before his colleagues came in and finally, to his own disappointment, could make no sense whatsoever of the messages Spiteri had gotten.

Dario Grimoldi appeared his usual self from the outside, but inside, he was still in a rage about the way

The Maltese Dahlia

Spiteri had spoken to him the previous day. He glanced over at Said; in his mind, a perfect example of what he was talking about. Grimoldi had accepted before now that Said was reasonably attractive and could easily have had a husband and children by now. Why hadn't she? Who would take such a woman for a wife was the real question. Happy to show off her figure, make-up on every day, dressing provocatively... Grimoldi had seen that for himself one day, when Said had leaned across to get a file from his desk. She was actually wearing a red bra at work.

Oblivious to Grimoldi's disapproval, Said turned around in her seat. 'Look, why don't we go into one of the interview rooms and try and put all our thoughts together on this Arnaud/Debono thing?' Grimoldi and Sammut agreed and, after collecting three coffees, disappeared into Interview Room 3. Spiteri nodded at Said as they all trooped off. She knew where they were going; she encouraged teamwork constantly, as a way of not wasting time duplicating work, if nothing else.

***

Paul Sammut hadn't gone into work that day. It was the first time in many months that he had taken a day off and, as there was nothing pressing at the mortuary and he had such a major conundrum to deal with, he had called in to say that if needed, they could call him; otherwise, he wouldn't be in for a couple of days.

Sammut had thought long and hard about who on the island would have the money, connections, and chutzpah to ignore any "morality issues" and invest in his new business. It was obvious that he couldn't let Michael know, but it was equally obvious that the man who fit the bill was Nicola Tizian. He had had his reservations about contacting and then meeting with Tizian, but in reality, he had found him charming and attentive. Tizian appeared genuinely shocked when he heard what

Sammut was proposing but said he would give it some thought and look into the best way to bring things like that into Malta without attracting attention.

***

Thea Spiteri was delighted when she got a call from Daphne Arrigo, suggesting a lunch date. As she walked past, she knocked on the door of the interview room where her team was grouped and let them know she was going out. 'Have that bombing solved for me when I come back.'

Inside the room, Sammut looked startled; Grimoldi didn't acknowledge the Kap's presence, and Said gave Sammut a reassuring smile, along with a slight shake of the head.

'Right, where are we now with this, guys?' said Said. 'Will I give an overview and then you can add things as you see it?'

Grimoldi and Sammut nodded in agreement.

'Okay... A couple of years ago, Enemalta management started to suspect that the money coming in on certain accounts didn't even remotely match estimated usage. Their own Protection Services unit investigated the goings-on and found out that tampered meters were being installed—usually in businesses, but also in some houses—that had been altered to only meter forty percent of the actual usage... so the bill was only forty percent of what it should be; in return, the guys who fitted the meters got a five-hundred euro handshake. More investigation appeared to narrow the scam down to one employee. The police were called in and the guy, John Scippitto, was arrested. It seemed a straightforward-enough case until Scippitto found out that there was no plea deal on the table from the magistrates. Scippitto asked to meet with a senior officer; he had a story to tell. A secret meeting was organised to take place in the governor's offices in Carradino Correctional Facility. At the meeting, Scippitto told police that he was just the tip of the iceberg, something that they had suspected anyway. Scippitto named two or three of the top managers in Enemalta as being involved, including Arnaud, and said he had documentation to back up his story. He went on to say that a couple of prominent politicians were involved, along with a "well-known local Mafia figure." He added that he had been promised that if he kept his mouth shut, a plea deal would be quietly put in place and he would get a very light sentence— possibly even no prison time. When he found out that he had been set up and there was no deal, he decided he was going to do a deal of his own. The police asked for the documentation incriminating Arnaud; then they would discuss immunity, as long as Scippitto gave up the politicians and gangster as well. Scippitto agreed and told them where the documents were. Police recovered them that afternoon. They then spoke to the magistrate, immunity was agreed, and they phoned the prison governor to tell him to inform Scippitto that a deal was on the table, and that they would be arriving at eight a.m. the following morning to take him to a safe house. As we now know, that morning's secret meeting wasn't so secret and Scippitto was found stabbed to death in his cell that night, with his tongue cut out and forced into his anus. Lovely sight, I'm sure.

'So, on first thoughts, who would you guys say the "mafia" figure mentioned is likely to be?'

Both men said 'Tizian' in unison.

'Agreed, and it's also common knowledge that Tizian and Debono are "close"… so he's not likely to give up Debono's name; or any other for that matter. And, if it isn't Tizian who's involved, who else on this island has it in them to car bomb someone on a main road? Finally, either way, Inspector Spiteri made it clear: our job is to see if we can find a link to Debono, not Tizian. In other words, is Debono the politician Scippitto was talking about—while he still could talk, that is?'

Grimoldi was the first to speak. 'There's nothing I can see in Arnaud's phone records to link him.'

'...and nothing in his bank statements either,' added Sammut.

'What about company records? Are Tizian and Debono both connected to any companies?'

Grimoldi and Sammut both shrugged. Said said, 'Why don't we look at that, then?'

Spiteri's team would soon find out that they were on the right road, just going in the wrong direction.

CHAPTER 10

Dan's Diner, situated in a back street near the remains of Tigne Fort, was an ideal place to meet, as far as Thea Spiteri was concerned. Parking wasn't difficult, it was usually reasonably quiet, it sold excellent local wine, and did a lunchtime portion of Bragjoli that was, in Arrigo's words, "to die for." Spiteri had arrived first and Arrigo a couple of minutes later. The two friends started laughing in unison about the way their last meeting had gone. Two Bragjoli and two glasses of red wine were duly ordered; Arrigo got down to business.

'The body parts business story isn't going away, Thea.'

'I promise you, Daphne, all joking aside. I haven't found one shred of evidence; if anything, the opposite, in fact. Just what is a "body parts business" anyway? I can't see how it works; too many people would need to be involved.'

'Well, I'm glad you asked that. I've been doing some research, and guess what? There's a link to here.'

'Are you serious?'

'Yes.

Daphne Arrigo took a quick sip of the wine that had just arrived. 'Right, listen to this: from *The Washington Post*, January 2006. "Hundreds of Americans are walking around with pieces of the wrong dead people inside of them. A macabre scandal has spread from a—*wait for it!*—body-harvesting lab in New Jersey to hospitals as far away as Florida, Nebraska, Texas... and Italy as hundreds of people discover that they have received tissue and bone carved from looted corpses."

'My God,' said Spiteri. 'How did it work?'

'So simple; genius, really. A doctor, who also owned the lab, approached dozens of funeral homes offering them tax-free, cash-on-the-day deals. They give him access to the bodies in their care; he extracts bone, tendons, skin... whatever. The body is buried or cremated and no one is any the wiser. This guy was actually shipping cooler container loads around the place full of body parts, tissue; et cetera. It's hard to believe, but it's true. Get this, eighteen thousand, nine hundred square feet of skin was used in 2003 alone. God knows how much is being used now with the advances in medicine since then. Anyway, more to the point, last year, three female corpses were exhumed in New York; all had had parts removed with one of them "missing about half its body." It's big business, Thea. I've got loads of stats, but I'll save you the details.'

'Okay, but what is the connection to here?'

'It's tenuous, but it's there. The guy behind the operation was called Mastromarino, a Corsican by birth apparently, and he's locked up. The point is, though, like I said, he distributed parts all over, and one of the hospitals was the Austin General Hospital in Texas, where a certain Doctor John Wayne was on the transplant team. He wasn't top man at that time, and there's nothing actually linking him to any purchases as such, but still. Anyway, I should find out more on Wednesday evening; I have a dinner date with a doctor friend. Don't ask!'

'It's interesting certainly, Daphne, and I'll look into it, although I'm not exactly sure how.' Spiteri paused momentarily. 'Does nothing else about the story raise your interest?'

The Maltese Dahlia

'Not really... what?'
'Mr Big.'
'What about him?'
'Corsican.'
'Oh come on, Thea. That's not Nico's line at all.'
'If you say so, Daphne. If you say so.'

***

Nicola sat checking the documentation he had carefully been putting together over several months. He was satisfied everything was in place. He picked up his mobile. 'Sandro, I'm going to make the call. Is everything as we agreed?'
'Yes.'
Tizian ended the call without reply. He put his mobile down and picked up one of the many mobiles that are lost every week in his clubs.
'Malta Freeport Customs. How may I help?'
'I have some information for you that I am sure you will be very interested in. Don't speak, just listen and take a note. There is a container sitting in Container Bay 3 opposite Kalafrana. It's registered to Mangion Machine Parts; the transit number is MVL 6598. It doesn't contain machine parts. It is due to be loaded tomorrow morning. Good-bye.' Tizian then dismantled the phone and discarded the parts and SIM card in three different rubbish bins as he strolled down to collect his car from outside Bar Barcelona.

***

Salvatore Grasso's hands were shaking as he put down the phone. *My God, I'm going to be rich. I can't collect the money myself; I might be recognised. Can I trust Mona?*

CHAPTER 11

Thea Spiteri was in her office an hour earlier than normal. She was determined to start looking into Duke Wayne's past and to check if her team was making any progress with the car bombing. Three phone calls would change her plans.

'Oh good, Thea, you're in. I wasn't sure if you would be yet.' Spiteri recognised Commissioner Galea's voice straightaway.

'How is your daughter, Kevin?'

'Good, thanks. Slow progress, but good.'

'Excellent, I think you...'

'Debono's been arrested.'

'What? What for?'

'I've just been informed by Customs. They got a tip off about a container. They seized it, opened it... Full of electric meters, presumably all tampered with.'

'Shit, what was he thinking?'

'It gets worse. There was also a sports bag containing explosives, more than likely the same kind that killed the Arnauds. If it can be proved it's from the same batch, he's on a double murder charge.'

'But what is the link to Debono?'

'The container belongs to a machine parts company. It has two directors: Pierre Arnaud and his wife.'

'Right... and...'

'When the company was registered, it had to say if it was a stand-alone company, limited or not, subsidiary of a larger company, owned any other companies... the usual. To cut a long story short, I got the fraud squad to have a quick look; they have the expertise, after all.'

'...and...'

'The company is a subsidiary of a holding company... owned by...'

'Debono.'

'Precisely.'

'He wouldn't be that stupid, surely?'

'Thea, we both know he's been corrupt for a long time. Sometimes people start to think they're invincible, or they just get careless.'

'I suppose so. Still...'

'Get your officers over to Customs House. He's not stupid; he knows the only glimmer of hope he's got is coming up with other names. Don't go yourself though, stick to this body parts nightmare thing; I can't begin to think of the headlines if the press gets a hold of that. Bye.'

'Bye.' Spiteri didn't have the heart to tell him it was already too late to stop the story, and if Arrigo could get any information on her "date"—*and if anyone could, Daphne could*—then the commissioner would be doing a lot of press interviews shortly.

Spiteri was still deep in thought regarding Debono when her phone rang again. She was surprised to hear Galea's voice again.

'The bastard has just called me!'

'Debono... how did...'

'No, the extortionist guy. Said he wanted to show he could deliver on his promises and acted "in good faith" by letting the operation go ahead before payment.'

'What do you think?'

'I don't know.'

'What did he ask for?'

'He wants thirty thousand euro now, or...'

'Or...'

'Well, he pointed out that he obviously has access to the hospital, and that unfortunately Jo Jo's body will reject the heart one night unless I pay up.'

'What are you going to do, Kevin?'

'Think. I'll get back to you. Bye'

Spiteri replaced her phone, her desire to find out what was happening at Mater Dei tempered by an awareness that Kevin Galea's daughter's life could rely on her judgement.

She could hear her team starting to arrive in the outer office and called Said and Grimoldi in to tell them about Debono. Spiteri finished up. 'I'm not going to brief you too much; you both probably know more than me about this case. You can let me know later how you get on. He'll be insulted by both your ranks; that's good, it will maybe fluster him, but don't be intimidated. He's the one in the mire.'

***

Nicola Tizian sat at the poolside of his converted farmhouse in Maghtab. Sandro, his contact at Valetta docks, had called him early that morning to say that the container had been seized, and he had subsequently found out that Debono had been arrested. His only concern now was that Debono would be stupid enough to implicate him, but he knew fear of prison was a powerful force.

Tizian finished his coffee and collected up all the documentation that was scattered over the rattan poolside table. When he knew Debono had been released on bail, he would immediately withdraw all the money from the Mangion Machine Parts company bank account and deposit a portion in Debono's wife's bank account: *an acceptable expense.* Both transactions would soon be tracked by *Pulizija* fraud officers, and that would be Debono finished. He glanced for a last time at the names of the various company directors' names and shareholdings, allowed himself a satisfying smile, and then dropped all of the papers in a metal rubbish bin and set them alight with his gold Cartier lighter. Nicola Tizian was now in sole charge of an electricity metering fraud that the authorities had only managed to scratch the surface of—and that they mistakenly thought they had now eliminated.

CHAPTER 12

Daphne Arrigo sat at her desk in *The Malta Times* offices in Valetta and pondered her dinner date with Mauro Cali the previous evening. She smiled to herself as she thought about how she had "accidently" bumped into him outside Mater Dei Hospital, how he had asked if she was okay, her apology, linked to her concern over a loved one who was maybe going to have to come into the hospital for a transplant. *I should have been an actress, really.* Cali had explained that she had bumped into the right person as he was 'part of the transplant team!'

Cali held out his hand. 'Mauro Cali.'

'Daphne, Daphne... Spiteri.'

The offer of dinner soon followed.

Mauro Cali was charming and attentive and, Arrigo had to admit, quite an interesting man, although there was something about him that wa*sn't exactly effeminate, but wasn't manly, either.* Cali explained that his family background was a bit obscure, but that he himself had been born in Brescia in Italy. His parents were poor but hard working and had sacrificed everything to help him get an education and move up in the world. He had studied medicine in the UK and Australia and practiced in Italy, UK, and, latterly, America. Daphne explained that she was a single parent and that she worked in the ads department of *The Malta Times*. 'Not quite at your level I'm afraid, Mauro.'

'Don't be silly. People are people; some are just more fortunate in life than others.'

'America... Texas, by any chance? I have relatives there,' said Arrigo.

'No, never that far south; Seattle and Chicago mostly.'

'New York?'

'No, I never even got the chance to visit. Maybe someday.'

'Wasn't there a scandal involving one of the hospitals there, something to do with trading in illegal body parts?'

Cali appeared shocked at the question. 'I've no idea! What a question!'

'Oh, it was just something I read somewhere. So, did you know Dr Wayne before you came here?'

'Only by reputation. He's a genius, you know. Top of his field. Very wealthy, even if he does like to eat in tacky steak houses.'

'Why do you think he came to Malta? Surely he could pick and choose.'

'He did. He chose here, as he has complete control over all of the workings of the transplant department. Controls everything from the most sophisticated equipment on the market to what paper towels he wants; he just doesn't need to pay the bills! He's determined to make a success of it; number one in Europe is the goal.'

'How's it progressing?'

'Very well; only the perennial problem.'

'Which is?'

'Sourcing suitable body parts and tissues, skin... that sort of thing. Gruesome, I know, but it is the line of business we are in.'

'And Mater Dei is having that kind of problem at the moment?'

'Not really, to be honest; in all transplant units, there seems to be a permanent anxiety about parts availability

The Maltese Dahlia

but Abela—he's the top man—and Dr Wayne seem to have it covered.'

Arrigo and Cali parted outside the restaurant and Arrigo's concern about a possibly embarrassing attempt at romance from Cali were dispelled when he held out his hand, shook Arrigo's gently, turned, and headed off into the balmy evening. Arrigo didn't know whether to feel insulted or not.

Daphne Arrigo had contacts all over the world; investigative journalism was a bit of an elite club, and those involved were happy to keep things that way. After dinner, she had gone straight home and called two of these contacts, one in Chicago and one in Seattle. She asked them both the same thing: would they check over the last few years and let her know if there had been any corpses desecrated there by having body parts removed, most likely for use in the illegal body parts business.

When she had arrived in her office the following morning, her voicemail was, as usual, full of messages, but two had what were, for her, disappointing messages: no body parts stories in either Seattle or Chicago. *Shit, that's Cali off the hook... I couldn't see it being him anyway... too, too... too what? I still can't put my finger on it.*

***

The Gordan Lighthouse sits proudly overlooking the Mediterranean to the east and to the west, the Ghammar Valley, home to Ghammar village itself, the Basilica at Ta Pinu, and the fruit fields that gently slope up to the village of Gharb. Every square metre of suitable ground has been cultivated for centuries, with the terraced fields containing a plethora of fruits and cereals. However, even the adaptable and hard-working Gozitan farmers could not cultivate more than a few metres of the rocky slopes leading up to the plateau where the lighthouse stood. It was on these slopes that the body of Susan

Vassallo had lain since the weekend. It had taken Joseph Melia, a construction worker doing some repairs at the lighthouse, several moments to realise what he was looking at as he sat on a collapsed sandstone wall eating his lunch. When he did realise, his lunch—both eaten and uneaten—lay in a pool of fly-covered mulch on the ground as Mallia rushed to his van to call the *Pulizija*.

The two officers from the *Pulizija*'s rapid response team, who turned up minutes later, were not the same two officers who had discovered The Maltese Dahlia, but they didn't need to be; the connection was obvious.

Even though Thea Spiteri was in Valetta when the call came through, she and Grimoldi were on site just over an hour later, courtesy of the *Pulizija* force's helicopter and an unsuspecting farmer who would discover some of his watermelon crop damaged in the morning.

'Looks like we have a serial killer,' said Grimoldi.

'Mmm, possibly,' ventured Spiteri.

'Possibly? They must be connected, surely.'

'I suppose so; it's just that serial killers seem to get more savage in their ways as they perfect their techniques. This doesn't seem to fit somehow.'

'In what way? It looks horrendous enough to me. Unrecognisable face, slashed body, multiple stab wounds, and it's obvious some organs have been removed. She hasn't been cut in half or sexually assaulted but...'

'How do you know she's not been sexually assaulted?' asked Spiteri.

Grimoldi paused momentarily. 'She has her panties on.'

'So?'

'Well, the killer's not going to put them back on after taking them off, is he?'

'Sergeant, look at this girl. What's been done to her... who knows how this guy's mind works, what he would or wouldn't do.'

The Maltese Dahlia

Susan Vassallo's I.D. and driving licence were in her bag. She was from Mellieha, a holiday town on the northeastern coast of Malta.

'Right. Dario, get a car to take you to the ferry at Mgarr, and another to pick you up from whatever ferry you manage to get. Speak to the parents; find out what you can. Had they reported her missing? If not, why not? I'm going to stay on here for a while; I'll catch up with you in Floriana.'

Spiteri took another look at the body lying on the ground. *She's no prostitute, but Grimoldi is right, there can't be two people doing virtually the same crime in such a short space of time. It's the same man; we must have a serial killer. Christ, not again.*

Spiteri walked away from the scene, sat on an upturned fruit box, and looked out at the bluest of blue sea. *Where are you when I need you, Matt?* Spiteri sighed and pressed a number on her speed dial.

'Hi, Thea,' answered Daphne Arrigo.

'Hi. How did your date go?'

'Okay. A little bit of background information, that's all. Nothing major.'

'Who was it with?'

'Thea, come on, I can't say. You know that.'

'Why not? Do you want to help me or what! Or are you only interested in your fucking story?'

Several seconds of silence followed before Arrigo answered, 'Thea, what's wrong?'

More silence. 'Sorry, Daphne. But there's been another girl killed... body parts taken.'

'Dear God.'

'I'll meet you this evening; a glass of wine or six definitely required. I'll call you.'

Spiteri then called Commissioner Galea. 'Commissioner, I'm on Gozo, there's...'

'Yes, I've heard, Thea. Bad?'

'As it gets.'

'Same killer as, as The Dahlia... God, I can't even remember her real name.'

'Letizia Corsu. Yes, it looks like it.'

'Body parts missing?'

'Yes.'

'Keep this between us for now, but you see the possible connection to your *other* investigation, don't you?'

'Well, the notion has flashed into my thoughts a couple of times, but...'

'This victim, how long has she been dead?'

'It's hard to tell; she's been lying on a hillside for God knows how long, and she's been badly mutilated. I'd rather let Paul Sammut make that call.'

'Paul Sammut. You don't see an issue there?'

'No, definitely not.'

'Okay, it's your investigation; I'll let you get on. Bye.'

'Bye, Comm...'

'Thea, one last thing.'

'Yes?'

'Your victim.'

'Yes?'

'Has her heart been removed?'

'I don't know for sure, but I'd say not.'

'Okay, bye.'

Spiteri looked back out to sea. *How terrible must this be for Kevin.*

CHAPTER 13

It was four-thirty p.m. before Spiteri and the rest of her squad had all returned to the squad room in Floriana. Spiteri wanted to catch up with everyone's progress but knew it would take more than half an hour and decided to give the team the option of staying on or doing a case review the following morning; all three opted to stay on.

'Okay, good. Michael, shoot over to the shop across the square to the mini market, please. Get four baguettes, or whatever anyone wants, and two bottles of Merlot.' Spiteri handed Sammut a fifty euro note. 'Be as quick as you can.'

By five p.m., the four colleagues were sitting in Spiteri's office having eaten their various choices; the three detectives were enjoying their first glass of wine. Spiteri was on her second.

'Right, let's get started. Letizia Corsu, The Maltese Dahlia. Anyone got any ideas at all; no matter how fanciful?' ventured Spiteri.

'Could it be suicide by chainsaw?' asked Sammut with a smile.

'Right, fine, no more wine for you, Constable!' Spiteri did not mind the humour; she felt it helped a team to bond.

'Okay, I take it the head shakes mean no progress?'

The head shakes turned to nods.

'Dario, how did it go with the parents of today's victim?'

'Jorge and Marie Vassallo; both distraught, obviously. Susan was their only child. Definitely not a prostitute; she was the manageress of an estate agents in Mellieha. They said she could be a bit of a wild child at times and that was why they hadn't questioned her not being home after the weekend. The estate agents' premises were closed for a few days, for decorating apparently, and so they thought she was just with friends. All they could tell me was that she was on Gozo for the fiesta weekend in ll-Qala, but they had no idea about her movements after that.'

'Il-Qala... wasn't that where you were, Michael?'

'No, I was in Sannat.'

'Pity. Okay, Sarah, what's the story with our esteemed ex-commissioner?'

'You were right about him not being pleased that Dario and I had been sent to question him. Started shouting about respect and suing the customs commission. He calmed down after about five minutes but didn't tell us anything worthwhile. He basically denied all knowledge of containers, meters, or the like.'

'Yes, and he nearly fainted when we mentioned bomb materials,' added Grimoldi.

Said nodded. 'That's true, but to be honest, the overall impression I got was that he was more scared than worried, if you know what I mean?'

Spiteri turned to Sammut. 'Michael, I knew it was asking a lot, but any words of wisdom on that voicemail I played you?'

'Sorry; but not really. Gyllenhall has been in a lot of movies, more than I thought, actually. I checked his star sign; it's Sagittarius... Whatever relevance that has to anything else, I've no idea. One small thing: the more I listened to the message, I don't think whoever left it is Maltese.'

'Really? I never noticed that.'

'Yes. I mean, it's not hugely obvious. It's not some, say, Scottish nut job... but not Maltese.'

'Let's leave things at that, then. I have an appointment anyway; see you all in the morning.'

Sarah Said deliberately messed in her bag in order to let Sammut and Grimoldi leave. 'He doesn't know about Matt, Thea... I'll speak to him.'

'No. It's okay. I'm fine. I can't go into a shell every time Scotland is mentioned, Sarah. After all, Maltese law is based on Scottish law; did you know that?'

'No, I didn't. Seriously?'

'Yip. Anyway, go home, enjoy your evening... and thanks.'

Spiteri looked at her watch after Said left. She knew she was due to call Daphne Arrigo but decided to sit for a while in her slowly darkening office, enjoying the rest of the wine. Spiteri didn't understand how alcohol could be considered a depressant. She felt the exact opposite: the warm glow helped to shift the dark thoughts in her head, allowed her to think of Matt and what might have been. She closed her eyes. *A Tale of Two Cities... It was the best of times; it was the worst of times... Why did you have to go, Matt... Was it to see your beloved Susan... Did I mean so little to you?*

Spiteri opened her eyes, looked down at her desk. The bottle of Merlot was finished and discarded, replaced by the special occasions Hennessey. Spiteri strained her eyes, tried to remember going and getting the brandy. She suddenly remembered about Arrigo and quickly looked at her watch. Ten p.m. *Shit.*

CHAPTER 14

Thea Spiteri was confused. Her bedroom ceiling looked a different colour, and the large fan that normally was the first thing she saw in the morning wasn't there. The room seemed noisier, too. She lived in the country but was sure she could hear buses and voices, lots of voices... and another noise, familiar yet muffled. Spiteri's mind slowly awoke. The noise was her mobile ringing in her bag.

'Spiteri.'

'Thea, sorry, again, I know it's early, but can you be in my office for eight-thirty a.m. please.' Commissioner Galea didn't wait for an answer.

Spiteri leaned back in her seat. The air in her car smelt stale and her mouth felt full of fungus. She looked at her watch. Seven-thirty a.m. *That gives me an hour. Coffee, wash, do what I can with my hair, buy a new blouse. At least I don't have far to travel.*

But Thea Spiteri wasn't laughing at the reality of sleeping in the car park outside police headquarters all night. *Matt, you've been where I am now. Help me.*

Spiteri walked briskly into Galea's office with no trace of fatigue or being dishevelled in any way.

Before she had sat down opposite the commissioner, Galea spoke. 'I got another call. It's now forty thousand euro since I've stalled unnecessarily and my daughter is doing so well. I recorded the call, but that's the gist of it.'

'What are you going to do? He obviously has some sort of access to how Josephine is doing, but I have to tell you, Commissioner, I've looked at the staff—not thoroughly, I haven't had the time—but there's nothing there and, as I said before, Paul Sammut says it's not happening. One other thing strikes me as odd.'

'What?'

'This kind of approach is not how the money is made in the body parts business. The money is made by selling to doctors and hospitals who don't really have an interest in where the parts come from; not by trying to extort money from the patient's family. How were things left?'

'That I was putting the money together but that if he kept putting the amount up, I wouldn't be able to pay.'

'Can't you move Josephine? He can't have access to every hospital.'

'To where? These patients are in special wards, and anyway, she can't be moved at the moment.'

'Have you managed to get any sort of information on the caller?'

'He sounds educated but excitable. He finished off by saying something odd. He said, "I want this money; after all, I don't want to break my wife's heart." So either he's trying to confuse us or he's a married man.'

'I'm not sure where to go from here, Commissioner.'

'I do. We're going to arrange a handover of the money and get this guy.'

'Are you sure, Kevin? What if he has an accomplice and sends him to the handover, and when it goes wrong, he…'

'Once the handover is in motion, Josephine's room will have armed guards put outside. There are no windows in her room, and only five or six people from the transplant unit have access. You've checked them all

The Maltese Dahlia

yourself, Thea. It's the only way. Right, what about this murder on Gozo; making any progress?'

'Not really. Sorry. Best we have at the moment is it's a serial killer and he's taking the parts as trophies or mementoes.'

'Mementoes?'

'Common practice apparently. They use them to relive the thrill of the kill.'

'God help us. Okay, just keep going; you'll get a break.'

Spiteri called Daphne Arrigo as she walked along the corridor from the commissioner's office.

'What happened to you last night?' answered Arrigo as an opening line.

'Sorry, really busy at work; didn't even go home.' Spiteri did manage to force a smile this time.

'Really, you must be shattered. Where are you?'

'I'm just leaving the commissioner's office, heading back to my own.'

'The commissioner's office... What's happening? Is it the body parts thing?'

'Nothing... and no! Do you want to meet this evening?'

'I can't, sorry... Meeting Nicola. How about now; a coffee in Guy's maybe?'

'Okay. Ten minutes.'

Arrigo was seated in a corner when Spiteri arrived. 'You were quick,' said Spiteri.

'I cheated; I was already here!'

'You're so devious.'

'Thea, I can't hold the story back any longer. *The Independent* is all over the murder on Gozo; I can't let them break the story first.'

'There is no story, Daphne. Hold off and I'll give you a story involving extortion, high office and, yes, body parts... but not the story you're thinking of.'

'Seriously?'

'Yes, I swear.'

'When?'
'Soon... in the next week.'
'Great. Thanks, but I was talking about The Cannibal of Malta story.'
'What are you talking about?'
'Two dead girls, insides taken out... you've seen *The Silence of the Lambs*. "I ate his liver with some fava beans, and a nice Chianti." '
'There's absolutely no evidence of that.'
'There's no evidence that he isn't eating them, either. The story is going in tomorrow, front page.'
'Oh thanks, Daphne... Thanks a lot.'

***

I am The Messenger
I have it all
I have meaning
I have purpose
I have love
I have the world

***

Paul Sammut had a good feeling about the way his plans were progressing. He was about to call Nicola Tizian to arrange another meeting, mainly to keep him informed of how things were going, but also to see how Tizian's negotiations were going. Sammut did still feel some unease over the morality of what he had started, but the Hippocratic Oath was one thing and business was business. Paul Sammut couldn't see why both things couldn't go hand in hand, especially if third parties benefited. He picked up his mobile.

'Nicola, its Paul Sammut.'

'I know. I never answer unless I know,' said Tizian, slightly unnerving Sammut.

'I've sourced some more materials. Can we meet... I don't want to discuss it over the phone.'

Tizian let out a low laugh. 'I see you are learning fast, Paul. Can we meet up next week? I have a lot on. I'll call you.'

'Yes, that's fine; I'll wait to hear from you. Ciao.'

***

Paul Sammut's son, Michael, also had something on his mind; he had to decide what movie he was going to go to over the coming weekend. He stole a quick glance at Said's thighs. *I wonder... What if she says no, though? The embarrassment.* Sammut jumped when Said suddenly turned and looked over at him.

'So, Michael, what do you have planned for the weekend? Another wild weekend on Gozo?'

'No. Why are you asking that?'

'God, Michael. It was only chat!'

'Sorry. I'm a bit frustrated about not getting the Gyllenhall thing. I'm having a quiet one this time, probably go to the movies.'

'Yea, to see what?'

'I haven't decided yet. Maybe just decide when I get there.'

'Are you taking a young lady?'

'No... I'm a free agent at the moment.'

'Right.' A few moments of silence followed before Said turned back round to her desk. Sammut was unsure if Said had been hinting about them going together; but he was still troubled about the previous weekend... one minute sitting happily with a girl, then blackout... then wakening to no girl and a bloody t-shirt.

***

If contentment manifested itself as a visible aura, then there would be a warm glow emanating from Mater Dei Hospital.

Peter Abela was reassured, if not altogether clear, on all the issues surrounding his dream. The transplant unit was proving to be a success, and there hadn't seemed to be any issue with the supply of parts. Abela couldn't put out of his mind the recent conversation he had had with Duke Wayne in the car park, but he had rigorously checked the entries that Wayne had put in the database for what his requirements were, and they had tied in with what had been delivered.

John Duke Wayne, although thrown by Debono's arrest, was equally as satisfied as Abela was with the progress his department was making. His disdain for Abela's ignorance of just how the success was being achieved remained in place; and just what Abela would do when Wayne had made enough money from his other business to move on, he hesitated to guess. One thing he did know was *that that sycophant Cali wouldn't be much of a help. A good doctor certainly, but with no management skills whatsoever, and business needs managed. End of story. Once Tizian gets back to me with the next step, I should be able to move even faster.*

Mauro Cali wasn't too concerned about the financial health of Mater Dei. He was content to be playing his own small part in the success of the department, he was working with a genius, he understood his role and not to question certain aspects of procedure and, most importantly of all, he was now in love for the first time. For Mauro Cali, life could not be better.

***

Like Mauro Cali, two other members of the Mater Dei staff were happy and in love. That morning, Salvatore Grasso had sat down with his wife and told her that by the end of the month, they would be able to start looking for a bigger apartment, maybe even a house, and that life was going to get better in every way. *I won't break your heart.* Grasso's wife didn't greet her husband's news with the enthusiasm he had hoped for, but Salvatore Grasso was unperturbed. His calls had gone well. He was going to make a lot of money.

Nurse Joyce Zirafi's lovelife was described as *It's complicated* on her Facebook page. It was complicated, but it was love nevertheless. Her boyfriend was a wonderful man and, although she loved Malta, he was going to take her to see places she had only dreamed of: Paris, London, maybe even New York. But best of all, he had insisted that they would be married on Cyprus, on the beach where Aphrodite herself rose from the sea. It wasn't too far away that her family couldn't attend, and he would hire a sailing boat and their honeymoon would be spent sailing the Aegean Sea. The downside was that he had a very stressful job in the airline industry which involved him being away for long stretches at a time; but once they were married, he had told Air Malta that he wanted to be based at Luqa permanently. Since he held such an important position, Air Malta had agreed, and the wedding was scheduled for 2016.

CHAPTER 15

Daphne Arrigo stole a furtive glance over the top of her menu at Nicola Tizian as he deliberated over what wine he would choose. Both he and Arrigo had ordered Spinotta L-Forn, and both knew that the thirty-to-forty-five-minute wait to be served would be worth it, as the restaurant in Ghajn Tuffieha, overlooking Golden Bay, was famous for its sea bass dishes.

Unlike Joyce Zirafi, marriage was something that Arrigo had never put much thought into; but she did now have a desire to have a child. She had no idea what Nicola's reaction, if that was suggested, would be. *Do I even need to discuss it? If he doesn't want anything to do with the child, then so be it.*

'A penny for your thoughts; isn't that an English saying?' asked Tizian.

'What... Oh, yes... Sorry... I was miles away.'

'Thinking about what?'

'Body parts.'

'What do you mean, *body parts*?' Tizian seemed irritated by the reply.

'You know that there was a murder on Gozo a week ago.'

'Of course.'

'Okay, but I don't imagine that you know that some of the poor girl's organs were taken?'

'No, I didn't. That is very interesting.'

'Interesting... Nauseating, I'd say.'

'Of course. I mean in the sense of who might do such a thing. What is Thea saying?'

'Nicola, I can't...'

'Daphne... what do you think I'm going to do? Can't you have a conversation without your journalist's hat on?'

Arrigo grimaced. 'Where is this coming from? What do you mean by that remark?'

Nicola Tizian reached over and took Arrigo's hand. 'Sorry. I have a lot of pressure at the moment. If you don't feel it's appropriate to talk to me, then okay.'

'It's okay, Nicola... I trust you. Thea thinks that the latest murder and The Dahlia killing are linked... a serial killer.'

'Interesting... and you?'

'Serial killer... maybe... but there must also be a link to the body parts scandal, I'm sure of it. Did you get anywhere with the Sicilian angle and The Dahlia killing?'

'No, nothing. I told Thea Spiteri I didn't see a connection at the time, remember. Was the girl on Gozo a prostitute as well?'

'No. Absolutely not.'

'I agree with Thea. It's the same killer; it has to be. But I'd forget about this body parts fixation you have... There is no body parts business. If there were, I would know of it.'

'No doubt you would, Nicola, but I'm not sure that that would be something to be proud of. Anyway, we'll see. I have an inside source at Mater Dei; I'll keep probing away.'

'Inside source... what do you mean, inside source? Who is it?'

Arrigo was again alerted by Tizian's mood change. 'Nicola, I appreciate you have pressures, but I'm going home now. Take your anger out on one of your paid female friends.'

The Maltese Dahlia

'Daphne...'
'Good night, Nicola.' Arrigo was back at her car and on her way home before she started to gather her thoughts. *Maybe a baby isn't such a good idea after all.*

***

Joseanne Scippitto was surprised that her husband, Daniel, had decided to go out to his local bar on a Sunday night. She didn't object to him going; he only went out occasionally and when he did, he never overindulged, came home late, or, as far as she knew, womanised in any way. It was more a case of her knowing how diligent he was when it came to his work as a bus driver with Arriva, and him not taking the slightest chance of being over the drink drive limit when he knew he would be driving children to school the following morning. It was true that he had seemed a bit distracted of late and that he was worried about his job, as Arriva had recently lost the bus contract on Malta. Maybe the fact that their five-year-old twin boys had insisted that they all sit on the couch and watch SpongeBob on the TV for the millionth time had made up his mind for him. Daniel lent over the back of the couch and kissed the top of all three heads curled up on the couch before walking out into the already dark night.

***

The overcast Monday morning was in keeping with the atmosphere in the room where Thea Spiteri and Dario Grimoldi stood beside the aluminium table as Paul Sammut performed the autopsy on the body of Susan Vassallo.

Even after having seen countless autopsies, Spiteri still found that it took some strength of will to watch a human being dissected.

'Blunt force trauma to the head killed her,' stated Sammut.

'Same as The Dahlia, would you say?'

'Not the same implement. In this case it was a rock, but yes.'

'Thanks, Paul. Can you give Dario a list of the organs and body parts that have been removed, as well as a list from the Corsu killing?'

'Of course.'

'I'll see you back in Floriana this afternoon, Dario,' said Spiteri as she turned to leave. As she reached the mortuary lab doors, Spiteri stopped. 'Paul, was Susan's heart removed?'

'No.'

'Was Letizia Corsu's?'

'Yes.'

'Thanks.' Spiteri closed her eyes tight as she pushed through the doors.

***

Sarah Said knew that Spiteri and Grimoldi were at the Vassallo post-mortem, so had allowed herself the luxury of bringing some Figolli into the squad room this morning to have with her essential first thing coffee. She walked over to Michael Sammut's desk, where her colleague was engrossed in the match report from the Sliema Wanderers game at the weekend.

'I didn't know you were a football fan, Michael.'

'Yes, I used to go to games a lot, but not so often now.'

'So how did your weekend go? Did you go to the cinema?'

'Yea, I went to see the original *Manhunter*.'

'*Manhunter*... Never heard of it.'

'A classic. The original Hannibal Lector, before *Silence of the Lambs*, and still the best.'

'I don't like those kinds of films. Why do people find it entertaining to watch slasher movies?'

'Please don't call them slasher movies. I agree that those are rubbish; I think they must be on to *Halloween 28* by now; worse than *Rocky*. But a good murder, horror, suspense movie; that's a different thing altogether. Don't tell me you haven't seen *Psycho*, the Hitchcock classic?'

'Yes, I have actually.'

'And?'

'Yea, okay... quite scary.'

'But did you enjoy watching it? Were you entertained?'

'Mm... good point. I'll need to think about that.'

'I'll let you know the next time a classic is on. I'll try and convert you.'

'Okay. Yes, I'd like that.'

Said walked back to her desk hoping that the thrill she felt inside wasn't obvious to Sammut. Sammut was thinking the same in reverse.

***

The Sergeant at the reception desk of the *Pulizija* station in Tarxien was having difficulty making any sense of what the clearly distraught woman in front of him was saying.

Joseanne Scippitto had dropped the twin boys off at school and then raced to the station to report her husband missing. After bringing a female officer out to help him calm the woman down, the sergeant had managed to establish that the woman's husband had gone to the pub the previous evening and not returned. Both officers tried to reassure her, but she was adamant that something terrible had happened. The sergeant pulled out a notepad to take down some details, more to give the agitated lady some reassurance rather than tell her that her husband was probably lying with some lady somewhere, or had slept in and gone straight to work.

'Okay. What is your husband's full name?'

'Daniel Scippitto.'

The sergeant looked up from his pad and then closed it over. 'Well, that was easy; case closed.'

'What?'

'Your husband was arrested last night, Mrs Scippitto. Drunk and disorderly, smashing a shop window, vandalising two cars, and assaulting two *Pulizija* officers while resisting arrest. He's probably in court right now.'

Mrs Scippitto was in a state of disbelief. 'Are you sure?'

'Oh, I'm sure alright. One of my officers is in hospital, thanks to your husband.'

'What will happen now?'

'He won't get bail. Not after what he's done to the officer.'

'I need to see him.'

'Look up the visiting times at Carradino, then,' said the now clearly unsympathetic officer as he walked away.

***

Commissioner Galea and his wife sat on the couch in their living room, looking up at Torri Grech, their son-in-law, with a mixture of surprise and uncertainty in their heads, as they had never seen him so angry.

'What is going on? Don't insult me by saying nothing. I go to the hospital to be with my wife, your daughter, and I'm asked who I am three times on the way to her room. There's an armed *Pulizija* officer stationed outside her door. I demand to know what's going on.'

Kevin Galea spoke up. 'It's very complicated, Torri.'

'Complicated? Right, so I'm too stupid to understand this complication, I assume? Why is my wife being protected like this?'

The Maltese Dahlia

'Someone is trying to extort money from us.'

Galea had spoken so matter-of-factly that Torri Grech hadn't really understood.

'Money? Extort? What are you talking about? What has this got to do with Jo Jo?'

'Before the operation was done, we were contacted by someone... someone offering us a heart.'

'What, are you serious? Why didn't you tell me?'

'We didn't want to worry you.'

'Right, I believe that. And...'

'He wanted thirty thousand euro.'

'You gave him it, right? I mean, you didn't haggle over your own daughter's life, did you?'

'No, we didn't haggle, as you put it. I told him we needed time. I started putting the money together but the next thing we knew, the hospital had sourced a heart and the operation was done. We didn't hear anything from the extortionist, but now he's come back. He seems to have access to the hospital. He now wants the money or he'll see that something goes wrong.'

***

Thea Spiteri was sitting in her office, feeling more and more repulsed as she read through the list of what had been removed from the two dead women, Vassallo and Corsu. She picked up her mobile and pressed Arrigo's number.

'Hi,' came in a rather subdued manner from Spiteri's closest friend.

'Everything okay?'

'You're not on to torture me over the Ghoul of Gozo headline, are you? It wasn't me, I promise. This new editor is a pain, learnt everything he knows from reading the UK *Sun*, I think.'

'What? No. I never even read it, to be honest.'

'Oh, thanks.'

'Daphne, your date with the mystery doctor; are you still on good terms? Are you planning on seeing him again?'

'Definitely!'

Arrigo's rather too enthusiastic reply alerted Spiteri. 'Trouble on the romantic front, I take it?'

'He's a pompous prick.'

'Right.'

'Thinks he can talk to me the way he talks to his female entourage.'

'Right.'

'I'm not phoning him; he can forget that. Do you know he... Aagh, you get the picture?'

'I don't think I would need to be the best detective on Malta to get it.'

'He's a bastard. I'm just going...'

'Daphne, can we meet? I'd like you to do something for me. You don't have to, but the story is yours if you do.'

'Is wine involved at this meeting?'

'No doubt.'

'Then yes.'

***

Dario Grimoldi sat in his car in the Floriana car park, overcome by a sense of joy and relief. He had decided to resign from the *Pulizija*. The previous night he had sat and explained to his wife that he just could not carry on in an organisation that did not seem able to see the real causes of the crimes that were now being committed on the Maltese islands. He had asked for her understanding. 'Ten years ago, child abductions, murder, prostitution... these were things that happened elsewhere, things we barely knew of. Now... now they are here, eating away at our society, our culture. What are we doing about it? We're pandering to it, instead of recognising and eliminating the causes... our lack of

The Maltese Dahlia

moral standards. A prostitute is murdered... find the killer... yes, but what is a prostitute doing here? The young girl on Gozo; okay, she wasn't a prostitute, but she stays out all night and her parents don't ask why? The woman killed in the bombing; dressed like a queen, all paid for by corruption. No, my real work cannot be done within the confines of this new Maltese society; I will restore the values that should never have been allowed to slip.'

***

Torri Grech was slumped into a chair. 'My God, do you have the money? Are you going to pay? Who's delivering it? Where? I'll do it... I'll kill the bastard.'

'Yes, we're going to pay. We're just waiting for the man to get back to us to tell us where and when.'

'You have to tell me everything from now on. Do you need any money from me? Can I help with that a bit; forty thousand euro is a lot of money.'

'No, but thank you anyway, Torri. It's just a case of waiting now.'

CHAPTER 16

Thea Spiteri was expecting her friend Daphne to be in full Boudicca mode when she turned up for their lunch date, but when Arrigo arrived, she was subdued if anything.

Spiteri didn't really want to spend her time talking about a lover's tiff but had to accept that that was what friends were supposed to do.

'Are you okay?' she asked.

'Yea, I'm fine. Sorry about earlier.'

'Sure?'

'Yes. So, to what do I owe the pleasure?'

'Daphne, I need a favour. If you don't want to do it, I'll understand.'

'Sounds intriguing. What is it?'

'I have a list of all the organs and limbs removed from the two recent killings.'

'Nice.'

'I know, but I've got to catch this guy, and...'

'What?'

'This goes no further for now, Daphne. The commissioner thinks there may be a link to your body parts for sale thing.'

'God, I knew it!'

'You told me you still have your inside source, right?'

'You want me to try and match the type of missing parts to transplants performed at Mater Dei.'
'Got it in one. Will you do it?'
'Bloody right I'll do it; what a story.'
'When will you meet him?'
'I'll call him, see when he's free. I'll get back to you.'
Spiteri gave Arrigo a copy of the list, finished her coffee, and headed back to her office. Arrigo fished her mobile from her bag and called Mauro Cali.

***

'Mr Abela. Mr Peter Abela?' a voice that Abela did not recognise had been put though to him by his secretary who had said that she didn't know who it was. 'They refused to say, but asked to tell you it was a matter of the utmost importance.'
'Yes, this is Peter Abela speaking.'
'Mr Abela, my name is Saud Al Nasser. I am Senior Advisor to King Abdullah of Saudi Arabia.'
'How may I help you?'
'I wish to arrange a private appointment with you, to discuss a private and delicate matter.'
'I see. Yes, of course; when would you like come?'
'As soon as possible.'
'When could you be here?'
'I am on Malta already, awaiting your convenience.'
'I see, in that case, come to my office at three p.m. today.'
'Thank you, I will be there. One final point, can you ensure that Doctor Wayne is in attendance?'

***

After her lunch with Arrigo, Spiteri had returned to *Pulizija* HQ and headed for her office. Said and Sammut were both shoulder deep in files, but Grimoldi wasn't around.

The Maltese Dahlia

'Where's Dario? Anyone know?'

'No. He was in for a couple of minutes earlier. I think he went into your office for a second, then he was gone.'

'What, he didn't say anything at all?'

Both Said and Sammut shook their heads.

Spiteri was now sitting at her desk reading, in disbelief, a six-page resignation letter from Grimoldi that veered from lack of professionalism in the *Pulizija* to the lack of leadership in the Church; from the way Maltese girls dressed to his intention to stand in the next election for the Morality Party which he was, apparently, about to form.

'Sarah, can you come in here, please?' shouted Spiteri.

When Said came through, Spiteri asked : 'Have you noticed anything odd with Grimoldi lately?'

'No, not really.'

'Not really?'

'Well, he likes to ogle; he thinks I don't notice, but...'

'Has he ever done or said anything inappropriate?'

'No; absolutely not. I think he's just a normal married man, if you get my meaning.'

'Unfortunately, Sarah... yes, I do.'

'Is something wrong?'

'He's resigned.'

'What, why?'

'Well, he's written a six-page explanation... but I still don't know.'

'Are you going to call him? Maybe he's had some kind of breakdown.'

'No. And even if he has, I'm not the person he would need to speak to.' Spiteri's phone began to ring. 'Okay, Sarah... Thanks.'

'Good afternoon ' answered Spiteri.

'Thea,' the commissioner said, 'the handover of the cash is on for tonight. I've organised everything but I can't be there myself, too personally involved; I'll be at home with family. I want you to be there, Thea. Let the heavy lot do any taking down that needs done, but you find out what you can, then come out to the house. Are you okay with that?'

'Yes, of course.'

'Good. Thank you. An Inspector Pietro Cassar will contact you shortly with the details. He's the officer in charge until it's over, then it's you. Good luck.'

***

At three p.m. prompt, Chief Executive Abela's secretary entered his office and announced the arrival of Saud Al Nasser. John Duke Wayne had been waiting with Abela, and so the introductions only needed to be made once. Coffee was served; Sandwiches offered, but declined.

'In what way can we help you?' asked Abela.

'His Royal Highness King Abdullah has heard good things about the capabilities of Mater Dei Hospital and Dr Wayne, in particular. Tell me, Mr Abela, what is one of a hospital's most important duties, would you say?'

'Professional patient care, the very best medical treatment available, value for money...'

'Money is of no consequence, Mr Abela; King Abdullah could buy the whole hospital if he wished.'

'Well... I don't...'

'Please, do not be insulted. I was only trying to illustrate that it is not a monetary issue that we have.'

'Just what is your issue?' Duke Wayne interrupted.

'The king has a daughter, Princess Lama Bint Abdul-Aziz; his only daughter. The princess has suffered from ill health for quite some time. Now it appears that she needs a transplant.'

'What kind?' Wayne asked.

'Well, it is not a transplant as such.'

'What is it then?'

'She needs .... a hysterectomy.'

'What's the big deal about that? Wait, what age is she?'

'Twenty-eight.'

'Why does she need this done? And tell the truth.'

'Mr, eh, Nasser... I'm sure my colleague wasn't implying anything... He can be rather brusque at times.' Peter Abela could envisage a golden opportunity going out of the window.

'I need your absolute assurance that this conversation is completely confidential.'

'Yes, of course.'

'The princess, unfortunately, like many young people nowadays, was a bit rebellious and lived in a way that was not in keeping with her position. Her father, the king, tried everything he could to keep her under control... and her, shall we say, more flamboyant adventures out of the media. Despite this, the princess found herself in an unfortunate position.'

'She's pregnant.' It was a statement rather than a question from Wayne. Abela squirmed but said nothing.

'She felt she could not go to her father with her... problem... and the man involved, a French playboy, assured her he knew of someone in Paris who would remedy the situation.'

'She had an abortion?'

'As you say, Dr Wayne, she had an abortion. Unfortunately, this... remedy... wasn't carried out in a hospital. In addition, these people were not aware that the placenta had attached itself to the uterine wall.'

'An accretion,' interrupted Wayne.

'That is correct. The princess started to, I think the expression is "bleed out." To make matters worse, the princess has a blood type of AB Negative... rare. She haemorrhaged and lost a lot of blood... and the doctor, for want of a better word, did not have access to a supply. He left the pair in his place of work, supposedly to try and get blood supplies, and never returned. Thankfully, the gigolo showed his first piece of clear thinking and called our embassy... Everything was taken care of from that point. Unfortunately, internal medical problems could not be taken care of so easily. Hence my visit here.'

'You should trace the boyfriend and the so-called doctor... Have them charged,' suggested Abela.

'Mr Abela, they have been traced, tried and convicted... and punished.'

Neither Abela nor Wayne saw the need to pursue that line of conversation.

'Well, Mr Nasser, although this is not exactly what this specialised unit does, I'm sure we will be able to accommodate you in some way; I'm sure that—'said Abela.

Duke Wayne interrupted Abela before he said anything stupid. 'Mr Nasser, tell the king that his daughter can be brought here anytime that he requires. I would suggest immediately, under the circumstances. There will be no paperwork involved and no formal fee notice issued.'

'Well, we'll need...' Abela stopped under the glare of Wayne's stare.

'I will carry out the operation myself. One nurse and one other doctor will need to be in attendance, but they will not know the identity of the patient. Am I right in thinking that these are the kind of assurances you wanted?'

'I see that you are more than just a great surgeon, Doctor Wayne; so what can my king do to repay such generosity?'

'Two things: There are advances in medicine and medical equipment happening all the time; we have only the best here in Mater Dei. Mr Abela and I will discuss what piece of equipment would be the most useful for the work my unit does. We will inform you of our choice in due course; you will buy the equipment, and have it delivered to Saudi... and then forwarded here. Again, there will be no need for paperwork.'

The Maltese Dahlia

'That seems a very generous and acceptable compromise, Doctor Wayne... and the second thing?'

'I'll think that over and let you know.'

Nasser looked hard at Wayne. A few seconds passed... then Nasser nodded his agreement.

'Where is the princess now?' asked Wayne.

'She is on the king's yacht, berthed just outside Valletta Harbour. There is a helicopter on board; I can have her here in a very short space of time.'

'Is she in pain, distress?'

'She appears to be peaceful, but she is heavily sedated.'

'Have her here in an hour.'

***

'Inspector Spiteri, my name is Inspector Cassar... Pietro Cassar... the commissioner tells me you are expecting my call.'

'Yes. I hear we have an interesting night ahead.'

'Let's hope it's fruitful. Okay, the details are that this guy wants the money in a silver-coated human organs hold-all; you probably know the type. He wants a uniformed officer to walk in the front door of St James Hospital in Sliema at seven p.m. precisely with the bag, leave it at reception saying it's for collection, and leave by the same front entrance.'

'Are the hospital staff in on this?'

'No. Commissioner Galea felt it was too dangerous, as this guy seems to have some way of tapping into anything happening in Mater Dei, so he's worried it's the same story here. Anyway, we have completely surrounded the hospital and the reception area is covered by TV cameras... as soon as the bag is collected, and this guy leaves the building... end of story.'

'What's in the bag?'

'Old copies of *The Malta Times*.'

'Ha, Daphne will love that!'

'What?'

'Sorry... private joke. Where and when will I meet you?'

'Do you know the old Cambridge Battery buildings, near Tigne?'

'Yes.'

'See you there at six-thirty p.m... My men are in place already, so no great rush.'

***

Spiteri whiled away the next couple of hours, trying to catch up on the endless mounds of paperwork that seemed to accumulate on her desk as if by magic. By five-thirty p.m., she decided she'd done enough paper pushing and contemplated trying to quickly grab something to eat before meeting Cassar. She was still undecided when her phone rang.

'Spiteri.'

'Inspector, it's the front desk here. I have three women here asking to speak to you.'

'Who are they? What do they want?'

'I would normally have ushered them away, but one of the women says she will only talk to you. She says she was at *Pulizija* Training College with you; Fiona Vella. She says it is a delicate situation concerning Mater Dei Hospital.'

'Put then in an empty office, I'll be right down.'

Thea Spiteri walked into the room where the three women were sitting in a row against the wall. Fiona Vella had only stayed a year in the *Pulizija* before going the way of most Maltese woman: a husband and children. Spiteri did recognise her, but she had changed a lot. *So have you, Thea... so have you. Who's right?*

'Fiona, great to see you. Is there something wrong? The desk sergeant said that you have an issue concerning Mater Dei?'

The Maltese Dahlia

'It's not Mater Dei as such, Thea... but somebody who works there.'

'Okay, and what is the problem with this person?'

One of the other women joined in. 'He's trying to extort money from us.'

Spiteri's heart leapt. 'For body parts?'

The three women looked at each other, bewildered. 'What?' asked Fiona Vella.

'This man. He wants money for body parts, yes?'

The three women still looked stunned. 'No,' said Vella.

'No? What does he want then?'

Fiona Vella looked at the two other women; they both nodded.

'Thea, all three of us, and we think more, have things that we don't wish our husbands to know about. Somehow, this man knows these facts and is threatening to tell our husbands.'

'Okay, is there anything you can tell me about this man? Would you say he's Maltese, British, Italian...'

'I know who he is,' said Vella.

'What? You know his name? How?'

'He worked for my father years ago. He's not simple but he's not the brightest, either. Anyway, he has a slight speech impediment, not bad, but when he gets excited, it gets worse. I've never come across anyone else with it; I'd recognise it anywhere.'

'So who is this guy?'

'His name is Salvatore Grasso.'

Spiteri looked at her watch: *I wonder. Maybe, just maybe.* 'Ladies, I have to go now, but I can assure you that by this time tomorrow, this will be over one way or the other.'

'Thea, we don't need a prosecution; we just need to know he isn't going to say anything.'

'Oh, don't worry. He won't.'

Spiteri escorted the women off the premises and ran to her car. She got to the Cambridge Battery just as

Cassar and his team were leaving to take up their positions around the hospital. 'Sorry, held up, but it may be for something that helps here.' Cassar and Spiteri took up positions where they could see the entrance to the hospital, as well as see the reception area on a video screen on Cassar's laptop.

At seven p.m. precisely, a rapid response car drew up at the hospital entrance and an officer got out carrying a silver bag. Cassar and Spiteri followed his progress through the entrance lobby to the reception desk. He placed the bag on the counter, a few words were exchanged, and the officer left. 'Right, now we wait. Fancy a coffee?' said Cassar.

Nothing happened. There was a slight panic when Cassar's team realised that seven p.m. was the start of visiting time, but not many people even approached the reception desk, and the waiting continued. By nine p.m. the hospital grounds and foyer were deserted, with only the change of shift nurses and auxiliary staff visible in the gloom. It was exactly nine-oh-seven p.m. when Officer Scerri noticed that the silver bag was missing. 'Get into that fucking building now; find that bag!' roared Cassar.

Spiteri held back. She knew she would be of little use amongst all the other *Pulizija* charging around the hospital and its grounds. *Think Thea, think. One minute the bag was there, and then it wasn't. There were no people in the area except...*

'Pietro, it's a nurse. Check the staff rooms.'

Ten minutes later, Thea Spiteri found herself sitting opposite an apparently partially traumatised Joyce Zirafi.

'I don't understand. What am I supposed to have done?'

Spiteri looked at the trembling wreck opposite her. 'Joyce, are you actually a nurse?'

'What! Of course I'm a nurse. What kind of question is that? I usually work in Mater Dei, but I take shifts wherever I can.'

'The silver bag you were taking, what's in it?'

'God, I knew this sounded odd.'

'What did?'

'My boyfriend, he's very high up in Air Malta; sorry, that wasn't me trying to be funny. He sometimes has to receive very confidential documents. They can't come through the normal post, so he enrols the help of the *Pulizija* to get the documents brought in secretly.'

'He enrols the *Pulizija*... Joyce, what age are you?'

'What do you mean? I don't understand.'

'Joyce, open the bag.'

Zirafi opened the bag, looked in, and started to cry. 'I don't understand any of this... I want to speak to my mum.'

'Joyce, what is your boyfriend's name?'

'Salvatore, Salvatore....'

Spiteri stood up and walked to the door. 'Don't bother... I know the rest.'

CHAPTER 17

Commissioner Kevin Galea lived in a modest house in Pembroke. Spiteri had been to the house once before, only to drop off or pick up the commissioner and so never went inside. The commissioner's wife couldn't hide her surprise when she opened the heavy wooden front door and saw Spiteri standing there. It seemed to take a few moments for it to register with her who Spiteri was, then anxiety kicked in. 'Oh my God, it's not bad...'

'No, no nothing like that; the commissioner is expecting me.'

'Oh, sorry... He never said. Come in, Inspector.'

Spiteri was led into the tastefully furnished living room that looked out over the nature reserve that separated Pembroke from the waves of the Mediterranean that crashed against the limestone cliffs, no matter the weather.

'Hello, Thea. Take a seat, let me introduce everyone. My wife you know obviously, and this is my son-in-law, Torri, and his mother, Mrs Rita Grech. Everyone, this is my finest officer, Inspector Thea Spiteri. Thea, would you like tea, coffee... some wine, perhaps?'

'No thank you, Commissioner.'

'Thea, please... you are in my home; make it Kevin. Inspector Spiteri was doing some undercover work tonight; I asked her to come over when it was done and let me know the outcome.'

'How exciting!' said Mrs Grech.

'Not really; a bit sad, actually. '

'Tell us, Thea,' said Galea.

'Well, the drop took place, the bag was eventually picked up... and a nurse was detained.'

'Everyone, my apologies. I didn't want to worry you. Someone has been trying to extort money from us, on the pretext that he supplied the heart for Jo Jo.'

'Good God in heaven, I can't believe it' Mrs Grech exhaled.

'Anyway, an agreement was reached to drop off the money tonight; that is what Thea has been doing. Sorry, Thea... carry on.'

'Like I said, a nurse was detained. I actually feel a bit sorry for her, her boyfriend has been leading her on a merry dance; I don't think she's involved, other than being incredibly gullible. Anyway, I think it finally dawned on her that she was in trouble; she gave up the boyfriend's name soon enough.'

'Who is it?' asked Galea.

'His name is Salvatore Grasso, a small-time criminal.'

'No it isn't,' said Galea.

'What? I'm not sure I follow, Kevin.'

'His name is Salvatore all right... Salvatore Grech... Isn't that true, Torri?'

Mrs Grech screamed, 'What are you saying? Your own flesh and blood!'

'My daughter is my flesh and blood; he is nothing to me... not now.'

Four sets of eyes were now fixed on the crestfallen figure of Salvatore Grech.

'Say something,' his mother shouted.

Grech looked over at his father-in-law. 'How did you know?'

'The other day, when I told you of the extortion attempt, you mentioned forty thousand euro... I never told you that was the new figure. There was only one way you could have known.'

The front door bell rang just as Mrs Grech began to plead for some understanding.

'That will be two officers; they are here to arrest you. I suggest you get a good lawyer.'

Salvatore Grech was led from the house in handcuffs with his mother following behind in a numbed silence.

'Sorry, Thea... I was hoping I was wrong; that you would come here with another explanation.'

'It's okay; I understand. At least you know that the heart Jo Jo got was sourced correctly.'

'Thank you, Thea... for everything. Any progress with your other cases?'

'Not a great deal, but we're still working away.'

'Good. Come, I'll walk you to the door. There is one other thing.' Galea led Spiteri out into the hall leading to the front door. 'Commissioner Prodi from Customs called me today. The bomb materials found in Debono's container are a match to the Arnaud killing. The meter serial numbers match the tampered ones already fitted and Debono's fingerprints are on a Bill of Lading found in one of the boxes. When you have time, I'd like you to visit him, see if you can knock some sense into him. Much as I now abhor the man, I can't see the chain ending with him.'

'Yes, I know what you mean. I'll find time. Good night, Comm... Kevin.'

***

Criminals, even small-time ones, seem to have a sixth sense for knowing that something isn't going to plan. Salvatore Grasso had that feeling when he opened his front door at eight a.m. the morning after Grech's arrest. He also didn't need to ask who Said and Sammut were or what they were doing there. Mona Grasso didn't need to ask, either; she merely looked from her husband to the *Pulizija* and back to her husband before slowly closing the kitchen door.

Mona Grasso waited until she heard the front door close before putting her head in her hands and weeping in a way that only the destitute can.

***

Thea Spiteri had decided on a lie-in after the strain of the previous night's surveillance operation. She had phoned in and instructed Said and Sammut to go and arrest Grasso, and then lay back on her pillow. She listened to the sounds of the countryside around her; she heard the filter pump for her pool switch on as the timer clicked to nine a.m... and she heard the laughter of her lost love and his voice detailing his plans for the future as she lay in his arms. Thea Spiteri had trained herself not to cry anymore over the past; she concentrated on the present instead.

Spiteri leant over to her bedside cabinet and pulled over an A4 pad and a red gel pen. *Red for important!* She carefully set out her title: "Where the fuck are we with everything?!?!" *Nice heading, Thea... classy.*

In a strange way, the making up of a list of what her squad still had to deal with was quite a cathartic exercise for Spiteri. Her small list only contained two actual concrete cases: the murders of The Maltese Dahlia, Letizia Corsu, and the murder of the young Vassallo girl on Gozo. Spiteri had thought of putting the Body Parts rumour on her list but felt that the previous night's arrest of Torri Grech had closed that chapter. Spiteri did, however, put a third item on her list: a question mark. Spiteri still had difficulty with the whole notion of Debono planting bombs in cars, along with the idea that he would make such basic mistakes if he was involved in anything illegal. Spiteri lay back on her pillow and mulled over whether to have a warm or cold shower to help her through the day. Just then, the phone on the bedside cabinet rang.

'Don't tell me you are still in bed, you lucky bitch!' ventured an envious Daphne Arrigo.

'Long night. What can I do for you, Mrs Journalist?'

'Why, what was on last night?'

'Daphne, why are you calling?'

'Traitor! To let you know that I'm meeting with my doctor friend tonight.'

'Well, have a nice time, but the body parts thing is a non-starter, so you don't need to bother with that.'

'What? How do you know?'

'It was an extortion racket, people making out they could supply an organ, but it was all bogus.'

'Shit. Are you sure?'

'What do you mean "shit?" We have a deranged killer on the island. Is that not bad enough?'

'You know what I mean. Any update on the killings, incidentally?'

'No.'

'Would you tell me if there was?'

'No.'

'Bitch.'

Both friends were smiling as they hung up.

***

Peter Abela and Duke Wayne were delighted and relieved. The operation on the Saudi Princess had been a success; no one other than the selected few knew anything about the patient's true identity and King Abdullah had informed Abela, through Nasser, that he was so delighted with the way things had been handled that, instead of buying a piece of equipment for the hospital, he was going to pay for Abela's next project, a laser surgery department, to be created at the hospital. Abela could hardly believe his—and the hospital's—good fortune. All thoughts of a second condition had completely evaporated from his mind.

It had, however, not gone from Duke Wayne's mind. As the helicopter landed to transport the princess back to the royal yacht, Duke Wayne was on hand to accompany her back to the helicopter.

'Mr Nasser, can I have a word before you go?' he asked after seeing the princess was comfortably secured for the short flight.

'Of course, Doctor Wayne. What can I do for you?'

'Mr Nasser, the king's generosity to the hospital is overwhelming and I am sure that the people of Malta will benefit greatly from it.'

'Thank you, Doctor. I will pass your kind words on to the king personally.'

'Yes, but perhaps I could prevail on you to approach the king on another matter?'

'Oh, and what might that be?'

'Let's just say that I have another source of revenue, one that is very lucrative, and it is part of my, shall we say business strategy to expand into other countries, especially ones that are forward-thinking and who appreciate the need for secrecy.'

'I see, and may I assume that perhaps you would require funding for your business?'

'Yes, but the rewards would be there, for both the king and the country.'

'You mentioned a business plan; do you have a copy with you?'

Wayne smiled and tapped his forehead. 'It's all in here. I would only discuss it in a face-to-face private meeting.'

It was Nasser's turn to smile. 'I will pass the details of this conversation on.'

John Duke Wayne watched as the helicopter took off and veered away towards Valletta Harbour. *Fuck you Tizian and fuck Malta... I'm dealing with the big boys now.*

The Maltese Dahlia

***

That evening, Peter Abela and Duke Wayne had suppressed their concerns over each other's perceived shortcomings and had a night of unbridled celebration. A meal in a small Italian restaurant just off Republic Street in Valetta had featured more Bardolino than pasta, and both men were now ensconced in Rick's Jazz Bar and were, at Wayne's insistence, attempting to sample every bourbon in the club. Abela had retreated to the toilet some ten minutes before, and Wayne was amusing himself by looking at the people passing by outside and deciding what organ he would most like to remove from each. It took him a moment to clear his head and focus his thinking on a couple who had just walked past. *Cali and Arrigo, my my... Isn't he a dark horse.*

CHAPTER 18

'You're right, unfortunately.' Spiteri managed a wry smile on hearing her friend on the phone.

'As always!' Spiteri replied.

'Yea, my contact told me last night. The tracking of organs is rigorous. Everything is checked and documented. The organs don't just get delivered with the mail. There was duplication with one of the organs taken from Vassallo, but since it was a kidney, I don't see much in that.'

'Glad to hear it.'

'Any progress on the murders? At the end of the day, someone is taking body parts.'

'That's true; don't you know the name of your cannibal friend?'

'I never wrote that; I just wrote that cannibalism was a possibility, something that people were in fear of.'

'What people? It hadn't crossed anyone's mind till you came up with it!'

'What, not even yours?'

'No!'

'Well, it should have; a few years back, there was a guy in Russia who did the same thing.'

'Mm, I wonder if you could tell. You know, if you were served a cooked steak, could you tell when you were eating it, do you think?'

'Not sure. Let's try it.'
'Try it! How?'
'Go to McDonalds.'
'Oh, ha ha. Ciao, Daphne.'

With both murder enquires not seeming to be progressing much, Spiteri had decided to visit Debono whilst she had the time. She walked into the outer office. 'Okay, I'm going out to Carradino to visit Debono. Have you got everything you need for the Grasso case?'

'Yes.'

'What about Salvatore Grech and the nurse? Have you got their phone records, credit card statements, all that kind of thing?'

'It's all been applied for; probably be Monday now before we get it,' replied Sammut.

'Okay. I won't be back in today, so...' Spiteri said as she walked out the door.

Said and Sammut took that as a sign that they didn't need to hang around till the end of the shift if they didn't want to.

'So, Michael, what excitement do you have lined up this weekend?'

'Ah, well, about that...' stuttered Sammut.

Said looked at her colleague, uncertain what was wrong: 'Are you okay?'

'Yes, fine. Great. It's just that I was wondering if you would like to... you know... meet up... or something?'

'"Meet up... or something" means what exactly?' Said was enjoying Sammut's awkwardness.

'Oh, I was thinking maybe going for a meal, or the cinema, or...I don't know really.'

'Michael, are you asking me out on a date?'

'I suppose so. I know you're my superior officer, and older than me, but...'

'Oh, Michael... you certainly know how to sweep a woman off her feet!'

'Really?'

The Maltese Dahlia

Said smiled. 'Well, we can discuss that on the date; now get on with some work for another hour, younger, junior officer.'

Said and Sammut were both happy people; for the present at least.

***

Ex-Police Commissioner Debono wasn't receiving any preferential treatment in prison; if anything, there was a certain amount of disdain amongst the staff and unbridled joy amongst the other prisoners. Debono was being kept in solitary confinement, for his own sake, but, with bail having been refused due to the fact that further charges including murder were pending, the situation was beginning to take a toll on his mental health.

Spiteri was already sitting at a table in an interview room when Debono was led in. It didn't take long before his arrogance returned.

'Inspector Spiteri, I suppose that's something. I wasn't amused by the other officers sent; not amused at all.'

'It's not an amusing situation.'

'Quite.'

'You've been told the news of the tests on the container?'

'Yes. I'm being set up; it's obvious.'

'Who by?'

Debono appeared to be about to say something, then just shrugged.

'You do realise that this is now going to be a double murder charge, as well as all the rest?'

Debono looked Spiteri in the eye. 'Do you really think that I am capable of blowing people up; innocent people, at that?'

'Were you involved in the electricity fraud?'

'Not really.'

'What does that mean?'

'It means I turned a blind eye. That's it.'

'For a payment, I take it?'

Debono shrugged again.

'If you don't mind me saying so, you don't seem to think that the things you have done, even the ones you're admitting to, are that much of an issue.'

'Inspector, everyone in senior positions bends the rules, and I mean everyone. They wouldn't be in senior positions if they didn't.'

'Bend the rules, or break them?'

Again, a shrug was Debono's only reply.

Spiteri paused, waited until Debono looked straight at her. 'One last chance: who is behind all this? Who organised the bombings? Who are you afraid of?'

Debono turned to the guard. 'I'd like to return to my cell, please.'

Spiteri had no sympathy for Debono as she watched his almost-broken figure leave the room; but she did wonder who it was that instilled such fear, that even someone as powerful as Debono was afraid.

***

Kay Tonna was twenty-nine years old. She exercised daily, ate all the right foods, didn't drink any alcohol, and didn't smoke. The only drug she had ever taken was aspirin. Kay Tonna also needed a heart and lung transplant

Her parents were distraught as they sat listening to Duke Wayne explaining the situation; Kay herself was completely at ease. 'When can we do this, Doctor Wayne?' she asked.

'There is a far greater chance of success if we do both transplants at the same time, and that both organs come from the same donor. We just have to wait.'

Mrs Tonna started to wail and Mr Tonna nodded at his daughter to take her mother out of the office. He turned to Wayne. 'What are her chances of survival, Doctor? Assuming you can source the double organs.'

'Surprisingly good. She has all the right attributes for leading a healthy life; it's just unfortunate that there is this hereditary problem in the family.'

Tonna studied Wayne's face. 'I am willing to pay.'

'Well yes. Of course there are fees.'

'No, I'm willing to pay for whatever it takes.'

Wayne returned Tonna's stare. 'What kind of business are you in, Mr Tonna?'

'I'm involved in import and export; I import from all over the world.'

'America?'

'Yes.'

'I'm sure we will be able to do business, Mr Tonna, but for now, we wait.'

The two men stood, shook hands, and Tonna left the office. Wayne turned and looked out of his window. *Everything is falling into place, Dad.*

***

Dario Grimoldi had not started his mission as yet. Every evening, he sat on the marble stairs outside Burger King in Paceville and watched as the sordid spectacle unfolded in front of his own eyes. Young people from countries as diverse as Japan and Norway staggered their way from bar to club in a swaying parody of model-like sophistication.

Grimoldi had decided to not concern himself with people who would only be on the island for a couple of weeks; his quest was to save the young Maltese girls who were being dragged into this world of debauchery, turning their backs on a way of life that had sustained their ancestors for hundreds of years. Dario Grimoldi had also decided that the Sicilian and Corsican scum who had brought this evil to his island were not, as they appeared to be, above paying a price for their sins.

***

Mauro Cali was again delighted to have had a call from Duke Wayne earlier suggesting they go for a drink. He was even more delighted when Wayne added, 'Not a meal, though. I've got things to do later.'

Wayne opted for a small table in a window recess of a traditional Maltese bar close to the new Parliament Building that was being built in Valletta. Some of the more traditionalist Maltese, referring to its modern design, called it "The Cheese Grater," but Wayne and Cali liked it and saw it as a sign that Malta was moving quickly into modern times.

'So Mauro, are you still enjoying working at Mater Dei?'

'Absolutely. Why... there's nothing wrong, is there?'

'Wrong... No, no... I just wanted to make sure that you are content, nothing bothering you.'

'No, nothing... I'm very content.'

'That's good. I've told you how much I appreciate your expertise and how you get things done, as it were.'

'You have, Duke... although I'm not sure I deserve the praise sometimes. As you yourself told me, "Do what you have to do."'

Wayne sipped his Pinot Grigio, a drink choice that had, in a pleasant way, also taken Cali completely by surprise.

'Mauro, we have a patient waiting. She needs a heart and lung double transplant. I have been on to my... network... It may take time. I want you to do something for me.'

'Yes, of course, anything I can, John... Duke.'

'You referred a moment ago to the conversation we had before, in the steak house. Well now is the time. I don't want or need to know, but if you can meet this girl's needs, then you will benefit, and in more ways than one.'

'I see.'

The Maltese Dahlia

'Good. Okay, I need to go now. As I said, I have a lot going at the moment.'

Cali watched as Wayne disappeared into the throng of tourists milling about the streets and byways. *"In more ways than one?" What does he mean by that? What is he asking?*

***

A man sitting alone, with only a coffee, a phone, and his thoughts for company sat looking out at the impossibly blue sea. His phone rang. He answered but didn't speak.

'You said you wanted to know about who visits Debono?' There was no reply, but the caller could hear breathing on the other end of the line. 'An Inspector Spiteri spoke to him this afternoon.'

The line went dead.

CHAPTER 19

As is the case for most people, seven a.m. on a Monday morning was not Thea Spiteri's favourite time of the week.

This particular Monday morning was no exception, and worse than most. Spiteri stood looking at the blood-soaked body of her former boss, ex *Pulizija* Commissioner Debono, a strange mixture of anger and detachment swirling in her head.

'What happened?' asked Commissioner Galea, who had accompanied Spiteri to the prison.

'We're not sure. He was found like this when he was brought his breakfast at six-thirty a.m.,' said Prison Governor Scicluna, as he paced the corridor.

'Cameras?' asked Spiteri.

'Nothing.'

'How can that be?'

'The cameras were off for ten minutes between six a.m. and ten past. Debono wasn't a popular person in here, you know.'

'Meaning?'

'Meaning lots of people in here will be happy today.'

'It must have been a member of staff who switched the camera off.'

'There are a lot of clever people in here, Inspector. Maybe the circuit was bypassed, or the camera shut down remotely... I've no idea at this time.'

***

It was just before nine a.m. when Spiteri trudged into her office. 'Sarah, I'm sorry, but can you make me a coffee please? My head is about to explode.'

Said glanced over at Sammut but didn't move towards the coffee area; Spiteri sensed something was wrong. 'What is it?'

'There's been another murder. We've just been notified.'

'I know; I've been on it since seven a.m.' Spiteri poured herself onto her office chair. A few moments later, Said came in with a mug of coffee.

'Thank you, Sarah.'

Said stood and looked down at Spiteri. 'Don't you want to get out to the scene as soon as possible?'

Spiteri looked confused. 'Sarah, I've been... I just told you that.'

'You've been...to the University?'

'The University? What are you talking about?'

'A body has been found in the Student Accommodation Block, organs removed.'

Within two minutes, Spiteri and Said were speeding towards Malta University. Spiteri explained about Debono on the way.

'God, who do you think is behind that?' asked Said.

'Take your pick, but I'd say that it's connected to Enemalta.'

Room 6, Block B was a small room typical of student accommodations the world over: a single bed, table and chair, wardrobe. The difference with this room was that it resembled an abattoir's yard that hadn't been hosed down that day.

The Maltese Dahlia

The body of the young student was barely recognisable as her legs were covered by a sheet and her head and shoulders had a pillow lying across them. The torso resembled a casualty of war: someone disembowelled by a landmine. The body was sliced open from the base of the neck to the top of the groin and it appeared as if all of the internal organs had been removed.

'Sarah, you stay here; you know what to do. I'm going back to Floriana to tell the Superintendent, get things set up, and then inform the commissioner; really make his day.'

Spiteri issued some further instructions to the uniformed officers who were in attendance, then headed for her car.

'Inspector.'

Spiteri turned. 'Dario, what are you doing here?' Grimoldi had a haunted look about him that Spiteri had never seen before. 'Are you feeling okay?'

'Yes, I'm fine. I'm sorry about my abrupt departure, but my calling is elsewhere.'

'Fine, so what are you doing here?'

'I'm attending a course here; I'm training to be a counsellor.'

Spiteri barely acknowledged Grimoldi's reply; she realised that she had never really taken to him while he was still in *Pulizija*, and even less so now. 'Right... good for you. Dario, I must go... Take care.'

Nevertheless, as Spiteri drove back to Floriana, she thought it strange that Grimoldi hadn't even asked what all the *Pulizija* activity was about. *Very strange indeed.*

***

Michael Sammut was alone in the office, which he felt was just as well. He had two subjects occupying his mind, leaving no room for paperwork duties. The first thing he couldn't understand was the odd way his father seemed to be behaving recently. There had been no arguments or signs of his obvious disapproval of his son, yet Sammut somehow got the feeling that his father was watching him. The second issue was the feel of Sarah Said's breasts. Sammut hadn't expected a particularly passionate first date, and he had behaved impeccably, but when they went to go their separate ways at the end of the night, Said had pulled Sammut into a tight embrace, and her firm curves electrified his whole body. Sammut had thought of little else since apart from his purchase of an original Jim Bowie knife, *As used at The Alamo*.

***

Peter Abela, Duke Wayne, and Mauro Cali were all sitting in Abela's office, delighted that the organ locator system had come up trumps once again and that Abela was about to call Kay Tonna to set a day for her to come in. Abela was aware that for many patients, news of an operation can be a mixed blessing, the chance of normality balanced against the risk of imminent death. He had no cause to worry when it came to Tonna, though; she screamed her delight down the line. Duke Wayne was already counting his bonus. Mauro Cali was trying to decide if he should attempt to have sex with Arrigo on their next date; he felt he was capable.

***

Michael Sammut was able to disguise his wandering thoughts so well that Spiteri didn't notice anything other than the young DC appearing to be working away.
'Is it the same killer, Ma'am?'
'Looks like it, Michael.'
'Would you like a coffee, Ma'am?'
'Michael, I'm putting you up for promotion immediately! That would be great, thank you.'

The Maltese Dahlia

Spiteri dropped her bag beside her desk, went over to her bookcase, and got out her bottle of brandy and put it on the floor at the side of the desk—the side hidden from the doorway. She collapsed into her seat and switched on her voicemail messages as Sammut arrived with her coffee.

Welcome to Voice Mail: you have two messages:
Message 1.   "Mark Harmon."
Message 2.   "I like students too."

Spiteri immediately looked up at Sammut.

'God. Right. Well, yes... Mark Harmon is an actor, the same as Gyllenhall, not as good in my opinion. He doesn't seem...'

'Michael... the second message?'

'Right, yes. No idea, sorry.'

'Michael, this latest victim was a student; you get onto your computer and find out as much as you can about this actor, any links to the other guy, and especially see if you can make any sense of the two second messages. Work out a possible link...Stars and students? I don't know; anything... Do what you can.'

***

Duke Wayne had only returned to his office for a few minutes when he got a call from Abela telling him to go back to the office immediately. As he walked along the corridor, Wayne was praying that Tonna hadn't said anything about money to Abela, although he felt confident that he would be able to talk himself out of any awkward situation that arose. He would be wrong.

Abela wasted no time. As Wayne entered his office, he erupted. 'What in God's name did you say to the Saudis?'

'The Saudis? Nothing.'

'Wayne, I've just had a Saudi minister on the phone, telling me how offended the king is that you have approached him without showing him the respect of going through the proper channels and demanding that you will only deal with him face to face.'

Wayne was in a state of internal panic. He was uncertain over what Abela actually knew. 'Rubbish. I just told that Nasser bloke that I would like to meet the king. Put a business proposition to him.'

'What proposition?'

'To build a sister hospital to this in Saudi.'

Abela studied Wayne's face, tried to work out his motivation although he could see the benefits to Mater Dei of such an idea. 'Why didn't you discuss this with me first?'

'It was just a fleeting conversation. If they had gotten back to me, then obviously I would have brought you in, Peter.'

'The king is reconsidering his financial assistance.'

'Really, send the bastard a £3 million invoice then. What's he going to do, not pay it?'

'There will be no invoice at all sent now; your stupidity has cost the hospital a fortune. I don't know what the Board will say. I might not be able to save you.'

'Save me... Are you serious? I am this fucking department. If I'm not here, you have nothing, not even organs.'

'What do you mean by that?'

'You work it out.' Duke Wayne stormed out of Abela's office despite the calls for him to come back. Within minutes, he was storming into Cali's office.

'Duke, what's wrong?' asked an alarmed Cali.

'Wrong? That fucking moron Abela, threatening me, that's what's wrong. Give me Daphne Arrigo's telephone number.'

Cali was taken off guard. 'Daphne Arrigo?'

'Look, I saw you two lovebirds in Valetta the other night; very touching.'

'Do you mean Daphne Spiteri?'

Wayne shook his head in exasperation. 'Fine. Just give me her number, then!'

The Maltese Dahlia

'I still don't see what you need her number for?'

'She works at *The Malta Times*, doesn't she? Well, I've got a story for her.'

'Yes, but in advertising.'

'What are you talking about? She's their senior investigative reporter. Just give me her number.'

Cali jotted down the number he had under *Spiteri*, too deep in thought to even notice that Wayne had already left the room.

CHAPTER 20

"Saudi Shock" screamed *The Malta Times* headline. "A prominent member of the present Saudi Royal Family, King Abdullah's own daughter, was secretly admitted to Mater Dei Hospital last week, in order to have emergency surgery to rectify damage done to her during an illegal abortion attempt in Paris."

Peter Abela sat in his office staring in disbelief at the newspaper headline. *We're ruined. This must have come from Wayne. Surely he must see he's finished now; not only here, but anywhere.*

Duke Wayne, on the other hand, was delighted by the story and had no intention of working any longer as a surgeon anyway. Mauro Cali's interest in the story was twofold: the first being the repercussions for the hospital and the second the tagline under the story: by Senior Investigative Reporter Daphne Arrigo. *Why did she feel she had to keep that from me? Did she really want a relationship with me?*

Nicola Tizian, too, was reading the story. 'Quite a tale, Daphne. How did you get the information?'

He and Arrigo were sitting having an early lunch in Benito's, overlooking St Paul's Bay. 'Now, now, Nicola. You know I can't reveal my sources. Let's just say my American doctor friend gave me a good break.'

Tizian smiled. 'That's good.'

***

I am the Messenger
My love knows no bounds
My work will continue
My oath fulfilled

***

'Have either of you got any special plans for tonight?' asked Spiteri.

Said and Sammut looked slightly flustered before Said replied that she didn't and Sammut shook his head.

'Would you like to go for something to eat, talk over these three murders?'

Fifteen minutes later, the three murder squad colleagues were seated in La Tosca Pizzeria, their orders taken and a bottle of Chianti opened and poured.

Spiteri looked across at Said. 'Okay, Sarah. Go over everything we know about the three dead girls, but not too loudly. We don't want those two Valetta ladies in the corner having nightmares.'

'Three victims, all female, all under fifty, one a prostitute, two not. One definitely killed indoors; one killed outdoors and one, we think, killed indoors and dumped outdoors. All three victims had organs and/or limbs removed. All three killings may be sexually motivated, but none of the victims were sexually abused, as such. Of course, the Dahlia, Corsu, was mutilated so badly that it is impossible to tell in her case. None of the victims had taken drugs. One victim, Vassallo, had been drinking but wasn't drunk. There doesn't appear to be any link between the victims other than the manner of their deaths.'

'Thank you, Sarah. Are the messages I've received genuine or coincidence; a hoax maybe?'

The Maltese Dahlia

Sammut replied, 'I don't know. Other than the fact that the two people mentioned are actors, I don't see a link, and I have no idea what the second messages mean.'

'Do they have the same star sign?' asked Spiteri.

'No. Harmon is a Virgo, Gyllenhall is... I forget, but he's definitely not Virgo.'

'Sagittarius, I think you told me,' said Spiteri.

'Do we have one killer or two, do you think, Michael?'

'One. It has to be.'

'Sarah?'

'I agree with Michael. One.'

'And you've double-checked phone records, bank statements... spoken to everyone who knew the victims?'

'Yes.'

A few moments of thought passed. 'How many killers do you think there are, Inspector?' asked Sammut.

'Two.'

'Really... what makes you think that?'

'Two things. One: the ferocity of the attacks, although all terrible, has diminished, not increased, as is the norm. Secondly, two messages... three bodies.'

'Maybe another message will come.'

'Maybe. Anyway, let's leave things...'

'An anagram!' Sammut nearly took off from his chair.

'Go on,' said Spiteri.

'Stars, students... both start with S... two actors with odd second names... He's taunting us.'

Spiteri looked over at Said, then back at Sammut. 'And?'

'And what?'

'The answer. What is the answer, Michael?'

'I don't know... It's a theory.'

'Michael, it's at times like these, I wish I'd chosen to be a nurse.' Spiteri attracted the waitress's attention. 'Excuse me; can we have three brandies please?'

Said and Spiteri shared a secret smile as Sammut fiddled dejectedly with his napkin. 'Michael.' Sammut reluctantly looked up. 'Good work. It shows you're thinking. If you can work that anagram out, I'll personally phone your dad! How is he anyway?'

'Odd.'

'Nothing new there, then! Right, one last thing before we head off; when did you two start seeing each other?'

Neither Said nor Sammut spoke. Finally, Said spoke up. 'We went to dinner but...'

'Sarah, Michael... if I see that it's not affecting your work, I can live with it. If I think it is... then Michael, you will need to move. I'm not losing Sarah. Agreed?' Both colleagues nodded. 'And don't make it common knowledge. It's not really approved of.'

Both nodded again, and then Sammut got up and went to the toilet.

'How did you know?' asked Said.

'Because of the way Michael looks at you; it reminds me of Matt.'

Said leaned over and took Spiteri's hand. No words were necessary.

***

Daphne Arrigo was a few minutes early for her dinner date with Nicola Tizian and didn't see him sitting in a corner cubicle at first, as he had his back to a rear entrance that Arrigo liked to use, as it was nearer the car park and Nicola Tizian always sat facing the front door. Always.

As Arrigo approached the cubicle, she could see that Tizian was on his mobile phone. She knew her boyfriend liked his privacy so she slid into the cubicle behind and signalled to the waiter for a glass of wine. *I could be sitting here a while!*

'How you got the parts is not my concern; I'm only interested in how much you want for them and how quickly you can deliver them... The paperwork has been taken care of. No one has questioned the, shall we say

The Maltese Dahlia

procurement methods or the costs... Ethical... What are you taking about ethical? Some people gain, some lose... That's life.

'The doctor? Listen, it was the doctor who came to me... at first, I thought it was a joke... Now I see it for what it is, a money machine, and one we can exploit... Listen, you are being well paid, but if you want out, then fine... You are not the only person who supplies... let's call them... *spare parts*, shall we... Okay, good. Ciao.'

Arrigo slid out of her cubicle and scurried back through the rear door. *What will I do, what will I do? Shit Daphne, you must go in.*

A few moments later, Nicola Tizian rose with a broad grin as Arrigo walked in the front door of the restaurant. 'Bella, you look beautiful, as always.'

'You sound happy.' Arrigo hoped her voice didn't give away the tenseness in her chest.

'I'm always happy to see you.'

'Extra happy. Concluded some massive business deal, have we?'

'What an odd question to ask, Daphne.'

Arrigo didn't think that Tizian had read anything into her question but she made a conscious decision to leave it. 'Nicola, I want Majjal fil-Forn with Bzar Ahdar Mimli... no arguments please!'

'My, you are forthright tonight; has Dr Wayne supplied you with another story?'

Arrigo tried to hide her surprise but gaped at Tizian despite herself.

'Daphne, don't eyeball me. Is that the correct expression in English? It is my job to know this island inside out. Wayne went to Debono months ago with a business proposition; Debono brought me in on it.'

'A business proposition? What kind of business proposition?'

'Daphne...'

'You ask me all the time about what I'm doing,' Arrigo looked down at her lap, 'and now Debono is dead.'

'Daphne, enough... your imagination is out of control at times. Do you like him?'
'Who?'
'Wayne.'
'Not particularly.'
'What about Cali?'
'Who?'
'Doctor Cali. Wayne's right hand man, from Italy.'
'I don't know him. What is his role?'
'Nicola, enough...' Arrigo raised her glass, smiling; Tizian could only reciprocate, but without the smile.

***

Not far from where Arrigo and Tizian were engaged in their jousting competition, Said and Sammut were sitting in a bar, barely able to take in that Spiteri had seen that they were in a relationship so quickly.
'How did she know? It's unbelievable!' said Sammut.
'She told me you are infatuated by my beauty.'
'Really?'
'Well?'
'Well what?'
'Are you?'
Before Sammut could answer, a group of about ten young men and six or so women came noisily into the bar. The majority clambered about looking for seats while two of the group went to the bar.
'Let's go, Sarah. It will be easier to talk somewhere quieter.'
'Michael, Michael Sammut... Governor of Gozo!'
Said turned and looked at one of the men at the bar, his pleasure at seeing Michael obvious. Two minutes later, a boisterous Tony Farrugia sat down beside Said.
'And who is this vision of loveliness then, Michael?'
'A work colleague. Sarah.'
'What... a *Pulizija* Officer... I'd better behave.'
Said laughed. 'Yes, you'd better!'

The Maltese Dahlia

'Sarah, would you be interested in dumping this wimp and going to bed with me?'

'Tempting offer, I must admit; but no. Thanks for asking, though.'

Farrugia roared with laughter as he got up to head back to his friends. 'I like her, Michael. Better than that prissy cow you were hanging all over in Qala the other week.'

That night, Sarah Said lay in her bed, going over the day's events. Two things bothered her: Michael Sammut was obviously too embarrassed to introduce her as his girlfriend. Said didn't know what the second thing was, but she knew it was there.

***

The following morning, Thea Spiteri hadn't even had time to get fully dressed for work when someone was banging at her door. Spiteri's house was reasonably remote, so she assumed it was someone she knew, but she was still careful as she opened the door a fraction.

'Daphne! Come in... what's wrong?'

'I've agonised all night about coming here, Thea, but I feel I must.'

'It's okay. What is it?'

'The three murder victims...'

'What about them?'

'They were killed for their organs and body parts.'

'For God's sake, Daphne, we've discussed this... agreed that's a non-starter.'

'It's true... What's more: I know who's behind it.'

'What... who?'

Arrigo propped herself up against Spiteri's kitchen table. 'Nicola.'

'What makes you think that?'

'I overheard him doing a deal; there's more.'

'What?'

'He said that he had been approached by a doctor to do it. He said he didn't want to at first, but then he saw how much money was involved.'

'What doctor?'

'I don't know. He never said the name.' Arrigo started to cry.

Spiteri walked over and hugged her friend. 'You've done the right thing, Daphne. Think of the poor victims.' Spiteri led Arrigo down the hall. 'You're exhausted. Take my room; get some sleep.'

Arrigo didn't argue and was soon sleeping soundly. Spiteri sat in her kitchen, trying to decide whether to tell Commissioner Galea or not; whether to bring back all the worry surrounding his daughter's new heart.

'Sod it.' Spiteri picked up her phone.

'Inspector Cassar, please.'

***

Unlike Duke Wayne, Mauro Cali liked to arrive at work early and give himself plenty of time to prepare for the day's schedule. He had gone through his usual checks this morning as well but his mind was elsewhere. He couldn't understand why Wayne would have been so reckless over the Saudi story, and he still couldn't come up with an explanation for why Arrigo had lied to him. Cali switched on his computer and went to make a coffee while it booted up. When he returned to his desk, his day became even more confused; the day's procedures had been cancelled. However, he hardly had time to take this information in when his phone rang.

'Mauro, will you come to my office, please,' was all that Peter Abela said. It wasn't a question.

A couple of minutes later, Cali was sitting in front of Abela; who was acting in a way Cali had never seen before, as he constantly adjusted his tie, and moved files from one tray to another for no apparent reason.

The Maltese Dahlia

'Mauro, I don't want you to be offended, or feel snubbed in any way, but the hospital board feels that you are not quite ready to lead the transplant unit at this time, but we will welcome your input on who you think we should consider. There are an obvious couple of candidates, but...'

'Stop! I've no idea what you are talking about... Doctor Wayne heads the department.'

'Not any more. He has resigned; before he was dismissed, obviously.'

Cali was numbed. 'Resigned? What, over that story in the paper? The reporter obviously got her information from someone, but not Doctor Wayne, I'm sure, and she sensationalised it, of course.'

'Wayne has admitted it was him, boasted it was him, actually. The Tonna operation has been postponed, obviously. Her father isn't pleased, I can tell you, and...'

The rest of Abela's word were lost on Cali. He couldn't believe that all that he and Wayne had worked for had evaporated in a couple of moments. Cali stood. 'There must be a way to resolve this; I'm going to speak to Duke.'

As he approached Wayne's office, Cali had no doubts that Wayne was in as he could, unbelievably, hear him whistling a Sergio Leone film theme. Cali didn't wait to be invited in.

'Cali, howdy. Want to meet in the saloon later, have a few beers?' Wayne joked.

'Duke, how can you be so relaxed? What are we going to do?'

'We? You can do as you please. I am moving on to better things.'

'You've got another post already?'

'In a way; you are now talking to the Managing Director of John Duke Wayne Enterprises... yes, sir.'

'Duke, surely you are taking me with you as part of your team?'

Wayne appeared genuinely confused. 'Part of my... What the fuck are you talking about? Listen, Cali, you effeminate little cunt, the only reason I've not drowned you in Ballutta Bay before now is that you served a purpose... no doubt getting great personal pleasure along the way. Get out of my office and if you see me on the street anytime, then just you mosey-on over to the other side of the road, partner—or I may just shoot you.'

Wayne returned to his whistling and packing; Cali quietly left the room.

***

'Sorry about my friend last night, Sarah... He was just drunk,' said Michael Sammut.

'That's okay. I thought he seemed fun, actually,' replied Said.

'What do you make of Spiteri's view on there being two killers out there?'

'Michael?'

'What?'

'Do you consider us to be dating?'

Sammut's face turned scarlet 'Well, I... do you?'

'I did, but you obviously weren't keen to let your friends think that.'

'No, it's not that. I'm not very experienced with women, to be honest, and I feel a bit intimidated by you.'

'Intimidated?'

'Not in a bad way; more a case of you being too good for me, really.'

Said smiled. 'You're a stupid idiot, Michael. Why don't we meet up tonight? Seal the deal, as it were?'

Sammut blushed again. 'I can't tonight, Sarah... Sorry. I have to meet my dad and then...'

'And then...'

'There's just a thing I have to do.'

'A thing... fine... Maybe some other time?'

The Maltese Dahlia

Said and Sammut both went to their desks, both unsure about what had just happened.

***

Dario Grimoldi sat in his darkened living room, constantly going over his next moves, making decisions on who to save, and who not. He knew it had been stupid of him to go to the murder scene, a risk, a risk that had backfired. If Spiteri checked on his story about being a student, he might have a problem. Grimoldi dwelt on Spiteri, the fact that she had embarrassed him in front of colleagues, took the side of the darkness. *Has she ever really known the pain of losing a loved one?* Grimoldi continued his planning well into the evening.

***

Spiteri, Cassar, and Galea had agreed that it would only be Cassar's team that carried the surveillance work on Nicola Tizian. Spiteri hadn't told Arrigo about the operation, either; she needed Arrigo to be acting as naturally as possible around Tizian. A couple of hours earlier, Cassar had called Spiteri and told her that a couple of his officers, posing as holiday-makers having lunch in Tizian's bar, had overheard him saying "Okay, tonight at eight p.m." to someone on his mobile as he wandered past the couples table.

Tizian had been followed from leaving his house to a small restaurant in Ghargur, and he was now sitting outside on the terrace, apparently waiting for someone. Spiteri and Cassar were sitting across the street in a Malta Bakery van that had been converted for surveillance purposes.

'Any joy with the murder investigations?' asked Cassar as he handed Spiteri a mug of soup.

'Nothing... Things couldn't get much worse.'

Paul Vincent Lee

Thea Spiteri was to find out over the next two nights how wrong she was.

***

I am The Messenger
No one can stand in my way
People may mock me
People may dismiss me
But no one will forget me.

CHAPTER 21

By eight-ten p.m., Tizian looked to be getting irritated that whoever he had arranged to meet had not shown up. Spiteri and Cassar were both sure that he was preparing to leave when a dark-coloured Nissan drew up; two men got out and walked over and shook Tizian's hand before sitting down at the table. The first of Spiteri's nightmares had arrived.

'Oh, please God, no.' Spiteri's mumble was barely audible, but Cassar knew something was wrong.

'What is it?'

'The two men.'

'What about them... Who are they?'

'One is Paul Sammut, our forensic pathologist... and the other one is his son, Michael. Michael is also one of my detective constables.'

'It doesn't necessarily mean anything, Thea.'

'Doesn't it? We suspect someone may be involved in selling body parts; that someone had been approached by a doctor to get into the business... then here he is, meeting a doctor with perfect no-questions-asked access to body parts... and the other man is a *Pulizija* Officer working on the case.'

'Still...'

'Forget it; we both know I'm right. To make matters worse, Paul Sammut is the one person I confided in... I took it as gospel when he told me that there was nothing going on at Mater Dei.'

A few minutes after arriving at the meeting, Michael Sammut got up, took what appeared to be an envelope from Tizian, and drove off. A few minutes after that, Paul Sammut and Tizian left in Tizian's car.

'Let's go. I'll need to talk to the commissioner straight away.'

As the surveillance van slipped away down a side street, Dario Grimoldi watched in amusement. *Tizian can't be that clever if he couldn't spot surveillance as obvious as that.* Grimoldi glanced back at the restaurant. *My former colleague, young Michael, and Papa, too... Interesting. Very interesting.*

***

Mauro Cali was still in a state of shock. It wasn't so much that Wayne was moving on without him; it was the fact that Wayne had obviously not valued the work that he had done, that was destroying him. Cali was uncertain about what he should be doing. *I'm in limbo, well, if there is such a place since the Pope threw that notion out along with half the other stuff.* Cali thought back to a few weeks previously, Pope Frances saying that the Church now accepted evolution as being true. *Ha, I wonder if we'll ever be able to transplant souls.*

Cali was still a bit bemused by Daphne Arrigo's part in everything that had gone on, but he still enjoyed her company and it wouldn't do any harm to just ask her why she didn't say she was a reporter. Cali decided to ask Arrigo to dinner that night.

'Yes, okay... That would be nice.'

Cali detected weariness in Arrigo's voice. 'Are you alright, Daphne?'

'Yes, I'm fine... but when you realise someone you care for is not the person you thought... well, it's difficult.'

'I know what you mean.'

Arrigo didn't miss the inference in Cali's reply. 'I know, Mauro, and I apologise. Unfortunately, I am in a business that turns people into... well, not very nice people.'

'I think you are a nice person, Daphne... if that helps at all. We all do things we regret in life. Have you heard that Duke Wayne has left the hospital?'

'No, I hadn't. Shit, that is partly my fault, no doubt... the Saudi scandal.'

'Don't worry; I think it was all part of a plan of his. He used us all. Anyway, we can chat tonight; maybe reassess our futures.'

Arrigo laughed. 'Yes, that should be interesting... A few wines required first, though!'

***

Peter Abela was also thinking about Daphne Arrigo. He partially blamed her for the crisis now enveloping the hospital. *She didn't even have the courtesy to come and talk to me before printing her sensationalist trash.* Peter Abela was not a man of violence, but he considered Arrigo's disdain for any sort of decency when it came to ruining other people's life as beneath contempt. Abela knew that his dream of having a world-renowned transplant unit on Malta was now ruined—and with it, his career. *You will pay, Ms Arrigo... I will make sure of it.*

***

The next morning, Sarah Said found herself sitting outside the commissioner's office with no idea why she was there. Spiteri had merely called her out of the squad room and they had come straight here. The commissioner's secretary picked up a phone on her desk on the first beep, listened for a second, and then said, 'Detective Said, you can go in now.'

'Sit down, Sergeant,' said Galea. 'I understand that you are in a relationship with DC Sammut, is that correct?'

'I'm not being flippant when I say this, Sir... but I honestly don't know. We've been to dinner and for a drink, but he is very reserved and so I find him difficult to communicate with on a personal basis. I suggested that we meet up last night, too; you know, go over things, but he said he was too busy.'

'Do you want a relationship with him?'

'I'm not sure... Can you tell me why you're asking me these things, Sir?'

Galea nodded at Spiteri. 'A week or so ago, we received some information that a body-parts-for-sale scandal involving Mater Dei Hospital might be operating. We were also told that Nicola Tizian might be involved. We put him under surveillance and last night, he met up with two people: Paul and Michael Sammut.'

It seemed to take an eternity for Spiteri's story to sink into Said's head.

'We're hoping it's nothing, but we can't take that chance. I've spoken to the commissioner and we feel that the best thing to do is have the Sammuts watched. The alternative is to suspend them both; but that would only raise questions.'

'And you want to know if I'll do it; observe Michael?'

'Basically, yes. If you don't, we'll understand and put another officer onto it... if you do, then personal feelings go out the window.'

'I'll do it.'

***

I am The Messenger
And what a message it is going to be
I'll whistle my tunes
And set my spirit free

CHAPTER 22

The beautiful sunny morning outside was a complete contrast to the atmosphere in the homicide squad room in Floriana.

Spiteri was trying to give off an air of normality, but Said appeared to have spent the night crying and Sammut had a look that Spiteri had only ever seen on the faces of people at a crime scene: a mixture of disbelief and haunted. 'So, Michael, what did you get up to last night?' asked Spiteri.

'Nothing really. I went out for a curry with some friends around seven-thirty p.m., then home. As a matter of fact, I haven't really felt right since; I was about to say to you that I need to go home... I know I'm going to be sick. Sorry.'

'Are you okay to drive? Would you like me to organise a lift?'

'No, it's okay; I'll be fine. Thank you.'

Said waited till she was sure that Sammut was well away. 'What shall I do? Do you want me to follow him?'

Spiteri pondered for a few moments. 'No, but call his house, not his mobile, in a few hours... make sure he's there. The surveillance operation is now covering Paul Sammut as well as Tizian; at least this way, we're on top of things.'

Inspector Thea Spiteri would never be so wrong; and in less than an hour's time, she would find out why.

***

'Are you going to be okay, Thea? You don't need to be here,' said Commissioner Galea.

'I'm fine, and I definitely need to be here.'

Galea nodded and walked over to Magistrate Xueres. Deputy Commissioner Grillo considered saying something to Spiteri but moved away, sensing a rage in the inspector. Only Sarah Said stood her ground. Four pairs of uniformed officers also stood in Argotti Botanical Gardens. All eyes watched carefully as both halves of Daphne Arrigo's body were placed in body bags and carried to the darkened mortuary van.

'Stop!' shouted Spiteri. 'Wait a moment.' Spiteri almost ran over to Galea and Xueres were standing. 'We can't have Paul Sammut doing the post mortem, Commissioner.'

'I'd thought of that, Thea. The body is being taken to St Bartholomew Hospital, out towards Luqa. A pathologist is being flown in from Greece.'

'Greece?'

'I couldn't take the chance on a Sicilian or Italian; not considering who may be involved here. What are you going to do now?'

'Go and see Tizian. Break the news, see what sort of reaction I get.'

'Do you think he's behind this?'

'Not even Tizian would have killed Daphne, not just for money anyway... but if he found out about the surveillance somehow, Michael Sammut for example, then maybe.'

Spiteri almost ran to her car before anything else distracted her. She knew that Tizian wouldn't be at work at this time, so she took a chance and raced to his home,

The Maltese Dahlia

screeching to a stop at the electronic gates that guarded his mansion in Maghtab.

She placed her hand on the horn and didn't take it off until one of Tizian's security staff appeared at the gates. 'I need to speak to Nicola Tizian; it's urgent!' Spiteri shouted, waving her *Pulizija* badge out of the window.

'Mr Tizian doesn't not see uninvited guests at his home.'

'Okay, then you can be responsible for the replacements.'

'What are you talking about, replacements?'

Spiteri sped back a few metres, then gunned her engine. 'The replacement gates.'

The guard's eyes flashed in panic as Spiteri raced forward. He held up his hands. 'Let me speak to Mr Tizian. What is your name?'

Spiteri observed a brief conversation taking place and then, as if by magic, the gates swung open. Nicola Tizian was at the front door to greet his guest personally.

'Thea, how delightful to see you. Come in. Please forgive that oaf at the gates; he's Russian, no more needs to be said.'

Tizian showed Spiteri into a vast living room and motioned for her to sit on a chair that gave her a view out over a large swimming pool and the grape fields beyond.

'Can I offer you anything? Coffee... tea perhaps... or something to eat...'

'Daphne's dead. Murdered.'

Nicola Tizian's facial expression didn't change for a few seconds, then Spiteri detected a slight twitch of his right eye. A further few moments passed and Tizian's face had taken on the pallor of the statues from the times of the knights: grey, hard, and cold. He sat opposite Spiteri.

'When did this happen?'

'We don't know exactly, but we'll find out.'

'Where did it happen?'

'Her body, sections, were found in the Argotti Botanical Gardens.' Spiteri's gaze was intense.

Tizian looked out onto his patio. 'Sections?'

'Daphne was cut in half in the same way that the girl known as The Maltese Dahlia was.'

'Exactly the same?'

'What do you mean?'

'It's not a hard question, Inspector. Was Daphne cut up in exactly the same manner as The Dahlia?'

'I can't say for certain, but I would say not. The Dahlia killing appeared more brutal.'

Tizian turned his gaze back towards Spiteri. 'Suspects?'

Spiteri returned the gaze; neither flinched.

'Ah, I see now. You suspect me.'

'Where were you last night? Did you see Daphne?'

'I was at work, where I was seen by numerous people; and I have not seen Daphne for two or three days; she hadn't even answered my calls. I assumed she was involved in some big investigation.'

'Did you discuss the projects Daphne was working on at any given time?'

'Occasionally.'

'Do you know Paul Sammut?'

'No. When can I see Daphne?'

Spiteri couldn't help but feel some compassion for Tizian. 'Nicola, I don't think that would be a good idea; remember her the way she was.' Spiteri sat for a few more moments. 'I need to go now.'

Tizian rose and showed her to the front door. 'Thea, do you really think I killed Daphne?'

Spiteri paused. 'I don't know, but I am going to find out.' She reached the top of the stairs above the driveway.

'Inspector, I did not kill Daphne, but I am going to kill whoever did. I know she loved you, and you her; if you really want justice done, then work with me.'

'I can't do that.'

The Maltese Dahlia

'Then do not stand in my way.'

Nicola Tizian stepped back and quietly closed his front door.

Spiteri stared at the imposing door for a few moments; an unexplained chill rippled her back. *This isn't an investigation anymore, Thea... This is a race.*

As she drove away from Tizian's home, Thea Spiteri wasn't sure that she wanted to win the race.

CHAPTER 23

Dr Costas Samaras had been secretively flown into Malta the following morning by private jet. He had gone straight to the hospital and performed his post-mortem. He was now on the phone to Spiteri, detailing his findings.

'She was killed by a stab wound to the heart; probably done by a large, hunting-type knife. She had a couple of small bruises on her arms, but nothing out of the ordinary. All other blows, and the dissection of the body, were all, mercifully, done after death.'

'Was she sexually assaulted?'

'No.'

'The dissection, how would you describe that; for example, I mean was she butchered, precision cuts... what?'

'Definitely not butchered although, like I said, a large knife was used.'

'Were any body parts removed?'

'No.'

Samaras and Spiteri spoke for a few more minutes and organised how Samaras was to submit his written report.

Spiteri sat at her desk and thought the unthinkable. 'Sarah, can you come through please?'

As soon as Said walked into the office, Spiteri could tell she had been crying.

'Sarah, close the door and sit down. What's wrong?'

Said attempted to answer, but a wave of despair engulfed her as her tears became wails.

Spiteri rushed round her desk, put her arms around her colleague. 'Sarah, it's okay. Whatever it is; it's okay.'

Said's despair seemed to subside and Spiteri brought her a glass of her emergency brandy.

'I called Michael yesterday afternoon, as you said.'

'And?'

'Michael wasn't there. His mother said he was away on business with his father; whatever that means. We chatted for a bit and then, quite unexpectedly, she asked me to dinner.'

'What... last night?'

'Yes. I wasn't sure what to do. I didn't want to call you because I knew you had enough on your mind. In the end, I decided to go. When I got there, Michael's mother had obviously told him I was coming, but he didn't seem that glad to see me. The dinner was a bit strained, so I decided to leave as soon as I could, without hurting Mrs Sammut's feelings. I needed the toilet and Mrs Sammut ushered me upstairs. As I walked along the hall, I couldn't resist the temptation of checking out Michael's room.'

'Okay... and?'

'It was like some sort of homage to violence. Posters, DVDs on the floor, a rope hanging on the wall, guns in a display case, a huge hunting knife lying on his bed, a set of...'

'Stop. What did you just say was on his bed?'

'It looked like a hunting knife.'

'Hold on a second.' Spiteri went to her desk and brought up the staff rota on her PC screen; Michael Sammut was off duty every night that a murder had taken place.

'Please, God, no,' Spiteri muttered.

'What is it?'

'It's nothing. What happened after you went back downstairs at the Sammuts'?'

'Nothing really. Like I said, I don't think Michael was exactly pleased to see me. He would know that I would be wondering about him supposing to be sick. What are you going to do, Inspector?'

'I'll need to think, talk to the commissioner... I'll speak to you then.'

As if on cue, Spiteri's phone rang. 'It's him,' said Spiteri to Said.

'Yes, Commissioner.'

'Hello, Thea. How are you feeling?'

'I thought after Matt that nothing would devastate me again, but...'

'I know... It's terrible. Are you sure you want to stay on the case?'

'Yes, without doubt; I'll grieve after I've caught this animal.'

'Did you speak to Tizian?'

'Yes. He was upset, I'm sure of that, but he's not the kind of man to give much away.'

'Do you suspect he's involved in any way?'

'At the moment, no; I do need to come and see you, though, Commissioner.'

'Urgently?'

'I would say so, yes.'

'Come here at four p.m.'

Spiteri had been surprised when Said hadn't left the room when she had taken the phone call but had put it down to Said's distressed state. Now she wasn't so sure. 'There's something else, isn't there, Sarah?'

Said could only nod.

Spiteri waited; she could tell Said was in inner turmoil.

'A couple of nights ago, Michael and I went for a coffee. Some of Michael's friends came in. I could tell he felt awkward. One of his friends came over; he was a bit drunk, but in a happy way. That night I was lying in bed; I couldn't put my finger on it, but something was playing on my mind. Last night, it came to me.'

'What was it?'

'The Gozo murder. At one of the squad meetings, you brought it up that Michael was in Qala, at the same fiesta as the victim. He said he wasn't there, that he was in Sannat.'

'I remember.'

'Well he was there, and he was in the company of a girl. I'm not saying it was the victim; I've no idea about that, but...'

'Why lie? I'm surprised he's not appeared today. I just assumed he was sick, but he must have known that you would tell me about last night.'

Said looked down at the floor. 'He asked me not to say anything. He had told me that his "illness" was that he was having some personal family problems. He said he was too embarrassed to say anything to you—and also unsure, in case you told his father.'

***

Dario Grimoldi had sat shaking for most of the night. He had gotten in around three a.m. and stripped off his clothes and scrubbed his whole body in a long shower. After the shower, he had pulled on a track suit, placed the t-shirt, jeans, and boxers he had been wearing in a plastic bag and locked them in the boot of his car. Grimoldi knew that he must have fallen asleep at some point, since it was now one p.m., but he was finding it hard to separate fantasy from reality. *Is this the only way? Am I making myself as guilty as them?*

***

By four-fifteen p.m., Spiteri had told Galea about the suspicions around Michael Sammut.

The Maltese Dahlia

'Right, I'll have him and his father put under twenty-four-hour surveillance. I'm also giving you access to as many officers as you want. We've got to finish this, Thea. *The Malta Times* is devoting the whole paper to this tomorrow; black borders around every page, prayers to the patron saint of journalists, whoever that is. This will be an international news story, Thea... intense pressure... we won't be given a lot of time, if any.'

Galea and Spiteri didn't know it at that point, but the killing of all four women, including The Maltese Dahlia, would be solved the next day.

CHAPTER 24

Mauro Cali was not an emotional man, but as he sat reading that morning's *Malta Times*, tears formed around his eyes and dripped onto the picture of Daphne Arrigo that took up the whole of the paper's front page. *Duke Wayne, the transplant department, now this. I need to leave here and start again somewhere else. I'll tell Abela today.*

***

Thea Spiteri had worked late into the previous evening, setting out a strategy and allocating officers to what was now four murder enquiries. A DS had been placed as the coordinator in each investigation, and they had to report back personally to Spiteri in her office at five p.m. each evening. She had decided to keep Said in the office, or out with her, in order to keep an eye on her.

As Mauro Cali was reading his paper, Spiteri marched into the Homicide Squad Room, driven by a steely determination within her that Daphne Arrigo's killer would not escape. She briefed her new personnel, then watched as they filed out of the office to take on their various allocated tasks. She then poured herself a coffee, not forgetting to throw in the two, now mandatory, paracetemol tablets and went to her own office. She immediately noticed her voicemail light flashing and reluctantly pressed the flashing button.

Welcome to Voicemail: You have four messages.

Message 1. "Ma'am, its Michael, Michael Sammut. I need to let you know that I won't be in for a week or so. Sorry to let you down. I read about your friend too. I'm so sorry."

Spiteri called through to Said. When she came, Spiteri played the message again. 'How do you think he sounds?'

'The same.'

'Mm.' Spiteri pressed the button again.

Message 2. I am the Messenger. You have two messages.

Message 1. "Brian Dennehy."

Message 2. "Don't you know how to catch a killer?"

Spiteri was about to ask Said if she could make any sense of the messages when Said suddenly shouted, 'Yes, I know it is... I just know it!' and ran from Spiteri's office.

Though momentarily taken aback, Spiteri chased after her. Said had run to her desk. 'Sarah, what is it?'

'The messages. I get it; I know what they mean. All of the first messages—they're all actors, right?'

'Yes.'

'Yes, but it's not the actors... it's the characters they play in real-life films. Give me a second,' Said said as she rattled away on her keyboard. 'Yes, yes, I knew it. The first actor, Jake Gyllenhall, he played The Zodiac Killer... The clue was "the stars"... astrology. The second one: Mark Harmon... He played Ted Bundy... famously killed students in their rooms... "I like students too."'

'Now this one: Brian Dennehy... he was in *To Catch a Killer*... Same as the clue... He's been laughing at us.'

'Who has.. Who was the film about?'

'John Wayne Gacy. Don't they say that serial killers want to get caught; they crave the recognition for what they do. Wayne is telling us it's him.'

'How do we know that someone isn't just setting him up?' asked Spiteri.

'One, for the reasons I've just given. Two, how would anyone else know about the Mater Dei body parts connection? Three, these killings only started after Wayne came to the island. Four; the clues all connected to films; everybody comments on Wayne going on about films all the time.'

'What Mater Dei connection?'

'Don't you see? The body parts weren't being taken to sell to the hospital, they were being taken for the hospital to use!'

Spiteri knew that everything Said was saying made sense, but she also knew that the theory equally applied to Michael Sammut, and it was the Sammuts who were dealing with Tizian.

Nevertheless, Spiteri ordered up two rapid response teams to go with her to Mater Dei, the Paul and Michael Sammut issue still eating away at her on the road there.

***

Commissioner Galea may have given Thea Spiteri access to as many officers as she needed, but Nicola Tizian had as big a network, and his network had no scruples when obtaining information.

'Tell me that again,' Tizian said to Bruno Pirlo, one of his trusted group.

'We've not got much, Nicola, but you know this story about body parts being available to the highest bidder. Well there's some truth in it. We got a hold of a guy called Grasso, a lowlife, trying to extort money for medical records. He told us that when he was arrested, he was asked about having involvement in offering body parts as well. He even said there'd been an arrest.'

'Daphne believed the rumours.'

'I know. I spoke to Joe Desmond at the *Times*. He said that the story had mostly gone away, but he knew that she was meeting some contact she had. I figured they'd maybe go to dinner. I asked around and she was in Il Bacco last night with some guy. They left about eleven p.m.'

'What guy?'

'They didn't know, but he was American.'

***

I am The Messenger
I am delivering my Message to the world
I will save lives
I will save my soul.

***

Dario Grimoldi looked at his wife across the kitchen table as she put his breakfast down in front of him. *Such beauty, such simplicity. You have always supported me; but would you support me if you knew the truth? Would you feel I had betrayed you?*

'You were home late last night, Dario.'

'Yes, working.'

'Do you think you are making any progress?'

Grimoldi studied his wife's face. 'What would you say love means, love between a man and his wife?'

'What a strange thing to ask!'

'Does it mean supporting each other, no matter what someone has done?'

'I suppose... but within reason. You hear of people doing such terrible things.'

'What if the thing, the bad thing, was for the greater good?'

'You mean like a soldier killing for his country?'

'In a way.'

'Then a wife would understand and, yes, support her husband.'

The Maltese Dahlia

'What about this man who has killed the women, cut them up?'

'He is an animal, a sick animal maybe, but an animal nevertheless.'

'Is he? Don't you need to know his reasoning?'

'Dario, what is this all about; are you feeling unwell?'

'No, I was just interested in your view.'

***

Spiteri arrived at the main entrance to Mater Dei Hospital in a cloud of dust and wailing sirens. She told the uniform *Pulizija* to stay outside but to be ready to come in if she called them.

Spiteri showed her I.D. at reception. 'I'm looking for Doctor Wayne, Doctor John Wayne.'

'I'm sorry, but Doctor Wayne no longer works here,' replied the portly nurse behind the counter.

'What? Since when?'

'It's been a little bit surrounded in secrecy, but he's gone. That is definite.'

'Do you have his home address?'

'I don't, but I'm sure someone will. They would need to get Mr Abela's permission to hand it out.'

'Can you get Mr Abela on the phone, please?'

The nurse picked up her phone and pressed a button. 'No response I'm afraid.'

Spiteri glanced at the nurse's name badge. 'Nurse Lombardi, this is a matter of life and death. Get someone out at this desk with Doctor Wayne's home address in the next two minutes or I'll have you arrested for obstruction.'

Nurse Lombardi stared for a second, and then got up from her desk and disappeared through a side door. A few moments later, she came back out and handed Spiteri a slip of paper.

***

Peter Abela had neither seen nor heard the two men approaching him from behind. He could remember opening his car door, then darkness.

He found himself now sitting in what looked like an abandoned farm shed, his head pounding and his hands tied.

'Mr Abela, do you know who I am?' asked Nicola Tizian.

'No... Do you know who I am!' shouted Abela. His rage was genuine, his fear greater.

'Why, yes. You are Peter Abela, the chief executive of Mater Dei Hospital. Am I right?'

Abela was confused; he couldn't put any of the pieces together. 'What do you want?'

'Just a little bit of information, that's all.'

'What information?'

'The transplant unit at the hospital; it is your pet project, is it not?'

'It was my dream, yes.'

'And your dream came true, Peter. You are a lucky man. You would do anything to make the unit a success, would you not?'

'Depends what you mean by anything.'

'Of course, let me be a little more specific. I understand that one of the biggest problems in your business is reliable sources of body parts; am I right in saying that, Peter?'

'Is that what this is about? Look, I told Wayne, I'm not dealing in any organs for sale deals.'

'Wayne. Would that be John Duke Wayne; he brought this up with you?'

'Yes, but I said no.... And it's still no; if that's what you're selling.'

Nicola Tizian's brow furrowed 'How many American doctors work for you, Peter?'

'American? Just one, but...'

Tizian interrupted, 'And just so we are clear, you are in sole charge of the unit, monitoring the in and outs of organs, et cetera?'

'Well, yes, but...'

Tizian nodded to a figure standing on Abela's left-hand side. Abela had been aware of his presence but hadn't actually seen him. He never would. Abela's pounding headache was dissolved by the single shot that tore through his head and exited just above his right ear.

Tizian walked to his car and opened the boot; the two large knifes he always had near were safely in place. He got into the car and sped off towards John Wayne's house. He had had less trouble finding out the address than Spiteri; his web of informers seemingly more efficient than "Malta's Finest."

***

Mauro Cali stood in amazement at the reception counter as Nurse Lombardi gave him a detailed account of the "disgraceful and insulting" way she had been bullied by the *Pulizija* earlier that morning.

'And all they wanted was Doctor Wayne's home address? That does seem odd.'

'I told them that they would need to speak to Abela, but he wasn't here either. The despicable woman then threatened to arrest me!'

'Well, you did all you could; just relax now. Is Mr Abela in?'

'No, I haven't seen him.'

'Can you let me know when he comes in if you can; I need to speak to him.'

'Yes. If I notice him coming in, I'll call you.'

***

Neither Tizian nor Spiteri were aware of the race they were in to get to Wayne's house first. If Spiteri had known, she wouldn't have been so surprised when she saw the tail end of what she was sure was Tizian's car disappear out of sight, just as she and the other *Pulizija* cars drew up.

'Shit,' said Spiteri.

'What?' asked Said.

'Nothing.' Spiteri envisaged the scene she was about to encounter in Wayne's house. 'Wait here, Sarah. You two come with me.'

On entering Wayne's hallway, Spiteri learned the truth of the phrase *the sound of silence*. Nothing; not a sound. Spiteri pointed to one of the officers and motioned for him to check upstairs. The second officer followed Spiteri into the lounge. Nothing except the muffled footsteps of the officer upstairs.

They went into the dining room. Nothing, not even signs of a struggle. Spiteri motioned for her colleague to check the kitchen; he returned at the same time as the officer from upstairs; both were shaking their heads. In a way, Spiteri was relieved, but she knew she would still have to find Wayne before Tizian did.

Spiteri left the house in a quandary over what to do next. Sarah Said walked over and asked: 'Nothing?'

Spiteri shook her head.

'I checked the number plate on that car there; it's Wayne's.'

'Sergeant, get that boot open please,' said Spiteri.

The boot sprung open, giving both Spiteri and Said a start, but it was empty apart from a rolled-up towel. 'Let's go. We've got to find Wayne.'

Spiteri had just reached her car when the uniform sergeant called her back. The officer had unravelled the towel and uncovered a blood-stained machete-like knife. 'Well done, Sergeant. Take it and get the blood tested straight away. Sarah, you go with him. Wait there for the results and phone me straight away.'

***

The Maltese Dahlia

Three days later, Commissioner Galea, Assistant Commissioner Grillo, Magistrate Xueres, Spiteri, and the uniform sergeant who had found the knife were all seated in the commissioner's office. Glasses of wine in hand, they toasted each other and the success of the press conference they had just conducted; even *The Malta Times* said that they would be printing a notice of gratitude in the next day's edition, praising the work of the *Pulizija* department.

'We still have to arrest them,' Spiteri ventured.

'I know, Thea, but the main thing is we've solved four murders—four particularly gruesome murders at that. The population feels safe again and the press is off our back for awhile. Do you think Abela and Wayne were in this together?'

'I'm not sure. Abela may have run because of the scandal. Neither of their passports are showing up anywhere. Possibly they're together... We just don't know.'

'What about the whole Tizian/organ parts thing? You know I had to stop the surveillance; too expensive, Thea... and we had Wayne.'

'I heard, yes. Well, I can concentrate fully on that now. I don't think Wayne worked alone; put it that way.'

CHAPTER 25

Thea Spiteri didn't think she drank too much. She was confident that she wasn't an alcoholic, just someone who drank to deal with stress, to help her sleep. *Nothing wrong with that.* Which made it all the harder for her to understand why she was standing in her kitchen at one a.m. and crying over the fact that she had dropped her last bottle of wine on the floor. She contemplated driving somewhere, anywhere, to try and buy another bottle but realised the stupidity of that thought. She bumped into the doorframe leading to her lounge, nearly knocking herself off balance, but managed to reach the couch without further mishap.

Spiteri had rarely made the comfort of her bed in recent days. She told herself that the couch was just as good, but the truth was that oblivion arrived at the couch and she welcomed its arrival. No Matt, no Daphne, no parents, no children; oblivion her only friend now.

***

The large numbers of *Pulizija* officers who had joined Spiteri's team to try and solve the four outstanding murder cases had now, just as quickly, dispersed to other investigations. Sarah Said sat alone in the squad room. She knew that the inspector wasn't coming in unless there was any update with the Sammuts and Tizian; and it was Michael Sammut who dominated her thoughts. Said's euphoria over being the one who had pinpointed Wayne as the killer soon dissipated when Spiteri had sat her down and pointed out some disturbing facts. Her inspector had been gentle about it, as she knew Said cared for Michael Sammut, but she was also a *Pulizija* DS and should not close her mind to the possibility that Michael was still a suspect. Yes, Wayne was the killer of Daphne Arrigo as the blood tests showed and, yes, he was probably the killer of the other girls; but that did not mean that Michael wasn't guilty of some other crime.

Spiteri had told her to think hard: She pointed out that it was Said herself who had spotted all was not right with young Sammut. She was the one who had discovered his apparent fixation for violence. It was her who had realised he had lied about the weekend on Gozo. She knew for a fact that Sammut was feigning illness. She knew for a fact that Michael, just like Wayne, was obsessed by the movies... and she now knew that she loved him.

***

Dario Grimoldi had watched the live news conference on TV with a mixture of disbelief and relief. Although it wasn't categorically stated at the conference that the killings were all carried out in order to obtain body parts, Grimoldi had heard the Mater Dei rumours. After the broadcast, he retreated into deep thought; something about the news was not right. He couldn't quite grasp what it was that was troubling him. He preferred to concentrate on what strategy he would follow now.

CHAPTER 26

Thea Spiteri surprised herself sometimes as to how it was she could rise early and be at work looking composed and professional.

As she entered the squad room she, like Said earlier, noticed how quiet the room seemed with only the forlorn figure of Said sitting there. 'Any news on Abela or Wayne's whereabouts, Sarah?'

'No, nothing. Interpol has sent confirmation that both of them are on their system now, though.'

'That's good. How are you today?'

'Fine, thanks.'

'Have you contacted Michael at all?'

'Best not to... Not at the moment, anyway.'

Spiteri nodded as she opened her own office door. Her phone rang before she had sat down.

'Commissioner.'

'Good Morning, Thea... beautiful day.' Galea was obviously still on a high.

'Good morning... yes, it is.'

'Right, I've just had word from Mater Dei, the chairman of the board. There's a substantial amount of money missing from their bank accounts.'

'Abela?'

'That's the feeling, yes. Wayne didn't have access.'

'How much is missing?'

'They're not entirely sure but over three million euro.'
'What?'
'I know. There have been a number of transfers to various accounts all over the world; just numbers, no names. I'm just letting you know, Thea. You don't need to get involved; I've got the fraud guys looking into it.'

'Okay, that's good. Any news on Wayne?'

'Afraid not.'

***

Spiteri had no sooner put her desk phone down than her mobile rang. She vaguely recognised the number but couldn't place it.

'Thea Spiteri.'

'Good morning, Thea. I hope you are well?' the dulcet tone of Nicola Tizian's voice sent a shiver down Spiteri's back.

'Nicola, what can I do for you? Is anything wrong?'

'No, nothing is wrong, but I do have a request.'

Spiteri was unnerved; Nicola Tizian's requests were normally commands; she was about to become more unnerved.

'Oh, and what is that?'

'Will you meet me for dinner?'

Spiteri was taken aback, rattled by thoughts of what Tizian's motives might be. However, this was a possible opportunity; there was a lot she wanted to know about Nicola Tizian. Her pondering took so long that Tizian asked, 'Thea, are you still there?'

'Yes, sorry Nicola. Someone brought a load of files into my office there. So, dinner... yes, if you like.'

'When would be convenient for you?'

'Any night; I don't have a hectic social life.'

'Then why not tonight?'

'Alright. Where and when?'

The Maltese Dahlia

'If I'm not mistaken, somewhere discreet on this occasion would suit you best, I think. Do you know the village of Gnejna?'

'Is that the one near L-Imgarr?'

'Exactly. There is a small traditional Maltese restaurant there. It is basic, but the food is marvellous. I know the family that owns it. It is called Ghagin U Ross; say eight p.m.?'

'Fine. I'll see you there.'

Spiteri hung up, her mind racing, trying to work out what Tizian wanted and why he wanted to meet her.

***

Paul Sammut, too, was troubled. He had read the coverage in the press and had seen the *Pulizija*'s obviously stage managed TV announcement; but he hadn't done a post-mortem on Daphne Arrigo. A post-mortem had obviously been done; but by who, and why not him? Had his meetings with Nicola Tizian somehow been noted, things deduced? He called Commissioner Galea.

'Doctor, how may I help you?'

'Commissioner, I'm looking for an explanation as to why I was bypassed on the Daphne Arrigo case.'

'Oh Doctor, Paul, my apologies. I meant to call you, but as I'm sure you'll realise, things have been hectic. *The Malta Times* is, shall we say, a little paranoid. They had all sorts of concerns that Arrigo's untimely death was linked to any number of investigations that she had either worked on or was still working on. To be perfectly honest with you, they don't trust the *Pulizija*, and that includes the whole justice system. They brought in their own pathologist.'

'Who was it, do you know?'

'I don't; someone from England, I believe.'

'England!'

'Apparently so. Anyway, there is nothing for you to concern yourself with. Now, I'm sorry, but I have to go.'

'Okay, thank you. Good-bye.'
Paul Sammut was partially appeased but felt he had to speed his plans up. He walked over to the bottom of his stairs. 'Michael!' he shouted.
'What?'
'Come down please; there is something I need to tell you.'

***

Although still nervous about what the evening may hold, Thea Spiteri loved Tizian's choice of restaurant: traditional stone walls, wooden bench seating, and food cooked on a log-fired stove. Nicola Tizian was already there when Spiteri arrived and had obviously chosen their table, set back from the other tables in a dimly lit alcove. Under different circumstances, Spiteri would have found it very romantic. As she walked over to the table, Tizian stood up and gestured for her to sit. He made no attempt to greet her with a traditional kiss. There was no menu to choose from; a weatherbeaten but spritely lady came over to the table, spent a few minutes telling them what was available, and took their orders: a shared antipasti of Bebbux BL-Arjoli, and both decided on Spaghetti BL' Arzell Friski. Tizian ordered a white and a red wine from the local Meridiana Estate, an Isis Chardonnay, and a Melqart, a blend of Merlot and Cabernet Sauvignon.

Tizian raised his glass. 'To Daphne.'
Spiteri dinked glasses. 'To Daphne.'
'I know you will be wondering why I asked you to dinner, Thea. The answer is quite simple: we had one mutual friend, and we've both lost her. We can deal with that individually or we can deal with it together. You feel we are different sides of the fence, I am sure, but I disagree. I want us to become friends.'

Spiteri hid her inner turmoil. She found herself touched by Tizian's words, but still suspected his motives. 'Nicola, I'm touched in a way by your words, but we are on different sides of the fence and I will never jump over that fence.'

'Tell me, Thea... The fence has another name, no? The law.'

'Exactly.'

'What is the law, Thea?'

'It is the rules we agree to live by.'

'Oh, and who decides these rules?'

'Society, government, the Church...'

'A nice trio indeed. Let us look at these rule makers, Thea. Society votes people into government, that is true, and here in Malta, the people engage well on election day, which is also true. But it means nothing, Thea. The government is a puppet, a puppet that flexes its muscle to impress the masses, while all the time relying on the steroids from global powers and global conglomerates. Then we have the Church; all religions, in fact. They preach of chastity, humility, and the evils of money... whilst at the same time procuring wealth that some countries could only dream of. I don't need to remind you, of all people, Thea, of the deceit in men's souls; even priests. So, these groups decide on the rule of law, what people can and cannot do. A simple example: last year, you could smoke in a bar; today you can't. Okay, that is not so important, but in Holland for example, they can not only smoke, they can smoke marijuana. A few years ago, the same thing applied across the USA; now, in five or six states, it is legal. Homosexuality, prostitution... illegal, yes... but on whose authority? Abortion, the right to die by assisted suicide... again, legal some places, but not in others. Further back, all civilised countries approved of slavery, now... need I go on?'

'Noone is saying that the law is perfect, but society needs rules or it will collapse.'

'Collapse? Let's talk about collapse. I read a very interesting article a while back concerning the biggest recent collapse in society and how it was dealt with: the banking collapse. In the UK, the government and the banks caused the economy to collapse, with laws being broken on a daily basis. Theft, corruption, insider trading, public assets sold to private enterprise; private enterprise that the self-same bankers and politicians owned. What to do? Easy. Put society into trillions of debt and blame immigrants and the poor. How many of the lawbreakers went to prison, Thea? Don't bother trying to guess; the answer is not one. But in Iceland, the problem was the same, only the solution was different. The bankers were jailed and the banks nationalised. Why? Because that was their law.'

Spiteri was taken aback, impressed by Tizian's passion. 'I understand what you are saying, Nicola, and I've no answers; but your arguments, although sound, cannot be used as a justification to break the law.'

'Thea, that is my point. Depending on who you are, where you are, and what age you live in, the law is just a figment of people's imagination... an ethereal notion that flows on the winds of chance.'

Spiteri couldn't find any words to combat Tizian's fervour; in truth, she was enraptured by this complex man.

'I'm sorry, Thea. I tend to go on too much, I know. Let me just finish up with this question: is it wrong to kill, is it against the laws of the government and the churches?'

'Yes, of course.'

'Then why is it that most people in history have been killed by government-approved actions, and in actions where both factions "had God on their side?"'

'Bob Dylan.'

'What?'

'Bob Dylan sang that.'

Tizian and Spiteri gazed at each other, then both broke into loud laughter.

CHAPTER 27

Sarah Said's heart leapt when she saw Michael Sammut's name on her mobile phone's screen. Her hands were shaking so much, she could hardly press the connection.

'Hi, Michael. How are you feeling?'

'Do you have my father under surveillance?'

'What... No. What are you talking about?'

'Some strange things have been happening around my father. He's not happy, and neither am I.'

'Michael, believe me, I have no idea what you're talking about.'

Sammut's tone eased. 'Sorry, Sarah; I didn't mean to have a go at you. It's just that there is a lot going on at the moment. I don't want anything getting in the way.'

'Okay. So, when will you be coming back?'

'Sarah, if I tell you something, do you promise not to tell Spiteri?'

Said closed her eyes, trembling at the thought of what might be coming next. 'Yes, I promise.' *Please God, not...*

'I don't think I'll be coming back.'

Said opened her eyes. 'Not coming back? Why not?'

'My father has established a business arrangement. He wants me involved.'

'Oh, what kind of business?'

'I can't really say, but I was never that committed to the *Pulizija*, you know that. This opportunity has the potential for big money, Sarah; I want to be successful.'

'Right, well... Will I see you again, Michael?'

'I'm going to be very busy... Maybe. I'll call you.'

'Yes, Okay... Do that. Bye, Michael.' Said never waited for a reply.

***

Dario Grimoldi walked through Paceville. It was still early, but it was better at this time, easier to pick the right one out. But Grimoldi's mind was focused enough on what he was doing. As he'd lain in bed the previous night, he remembered what was troubling him about the *Pulizija* press conference. He had to think of a way of revealing what he knew without becoming involved.

Some high-pitched screams from a group of barely dressed young girls stumbling out of Oasis caught his attention. He would deal with Spiteri tomorrow.

***

'Are you suggestion that it's okay to kill people, Nicola?'

'I'm not suggesting anything, Thea. Merely pointing out the facts. I thought the *Pulizija* liked facts,' he said with a slight smile.

'I think you killed Wayne.'

'You do?'

'I saw you driving away from Wayne's house.'

'And did you find Wayne's body in the house?'

'No.'

'So...'

'I don't know... Why did you have Debono killed?'

'Debono? How can you even think that? We had been friends since we were boys. Why would I?'

The Maltese Dahlia

'Because you were involved in the Enemalta scam; you couldn't be sure he wouldn't talk.'

'Thea, I was enjoying our evening, and I intend to go on enjoying it. I'm going to forgive this temporary sourness that you have introduced; you are *Pulizija*, after all. I will say only this and ask you to ponder it later. Who was it that brought Debono to your attention? Through Daphne, it was me. Correct?

'Who miraculously discovered the container at the docks? Customs Commissioner Prodi. Correct? Who did he then call? Commissioner Galea. Correct?

'Who told you to go to Carradino and find out what Debono was going to say? Galea. Correct? Debono used to be the *Pulizija* Commissioner. He broke the law. He was quietly retired on a full pension; no charges. Correct?

'Who walked straight into a senior political post and onto the Gas and Electricity Committee? Debono. Correct?

'Who was Debono's closest ally for years; who did he recommend to take over his job? Galea. Correct?

'Think back on our earlier discussion Thea, what exactly is The Law?

'And now, some brandy, I think.'

Spiteri was starting to see the fascination that had held Daphne Arrigo's attention. 'Tell me about yourself, Nicola.'

Tizian smiled. 'Do you want to know as a friend, or as a *Pulizija* inspector?'

Spiteri wasn't sure if the wine and brandy was clouding her judgement but for the first time, she could see Tizian as a friend. 'You decide,' she said.

'I was born in a town called Bastia, a sea port. My parents were honest people, so we were poor. By the time I reached my teens, I was determined that I wasn't going to stay poor. I started to steal; not from poor families, but from the homes and houses of the wealthy and from shipments going in and out of the docks. My exploits soon came to the notice of a man called Richard Casanova. Casanova was the head of the Brise de Mar, the Sea Breeze Gang; they got their name from the café in Bastia where they held their meetings.'

'Yes, you mentioned them when I came to talk to you before… Daphne was there.'

Both of their minds momentarily focused on happier times.

'Anyway, Casanova summoned me there; I was terrified. He asked me two questions: "How much are you making a week from my docks, garcon?"

I can't remember what my mumbled answer was.

"How much do you intend paying me for overseeing your enterprise?" he added.

My mind raced: 'ten percent' I said.

"Make that twenty percent, garcon… and you'll be able to walk out of here."

'I walked out in one piece.'

'Discretion the better part of valour; as the British say?'

'Perhaps.'

'So you are in the Mafia?'

'Thea, what have we just discussed? You need to open your eyes. Mafia, governments, multi-nationals, churches… they are all just different words for the same thing: money-making machines.'

Spiteri was about to interrupt but gave her head a slight shake as a wry smile crossed her face.

'What?' asked Tizian.

'Nothing.' Spiteri was still smiling.

'Tell me!'

'I was just about to butt in and say "but they don't kill people!" then I remembered Al Pacino's line in *The Godfather*: "who's being naive now, Kate?"'

'So Thea, now you; tell me a little bit about yourself.'

'Very simple really: no parents, no husband, no children… now, no friends. I always wanted to join the *Pulizija*… Here I am.'

Tizian gazed at Spiteri. 'Why no husband, Thea? You are a very beautiful woman.'

'There was someone once; it seems like a lifetime ago now... It wasn't to be.'

'Happiness will find you, Thea. I'm sure of that.'

'Really, why do you think that Nicola?'

'Because you are a good person. Daphne told me you were, and now I see it for myself. You only know what you think you know about me, Thea; as I say, open your eyes... and your mind; you may see me, and the world, in a different light.'

Spiteri didn't reply. She looked at this man sitting across from her, a man who represented everything she despised... and yet.

'Now Thea, I have to go. One of my colleagues will drive you home, and another will follow in your car. We can't have you breaking the law, after all. I've enjoyed our night, I hope we can do it again.'

'Yes, so do I.' The words had come out of Spiteri's mouth before she had properly thought them through; but on the way home, she realised she didn't regret them.

CHAPTER 28

Thea Spiteri lay in bed, wracking her brain, trying to find the correct words to describe how she felt. She had spent the previous evening at dinner with a man who admitted he was a criminal, at least linked to the Mafia, a man who, twenty-four hours earlier, she would have would have condemned out of hand. *But now...*

What had she to make of his views on life and the law, what should she do about his assertions surrounding Galea... and, most importantly of all, what was she to do about this feeling inside her, her desire to see this man again? Spiteri's alarm rang. She threw off the duvet cover... and only then realised that she was in her bed and not semi-comatose on her couch. Spiteri showered, had coffee, and set off for her office in Floriana.

Sarah Said was already in the office. Another sleepless night, thoughts of Michael Sammut and the promise she made him.

Nicola Tizian, too, was up and thinking about his previous evening's activities. He had enjoyed Spiteri's company and was disappointed that he had had to cut it short, but his meeting with the Sammuts was important.

Spiteri walked into the office and got down to work straightaway. 'You don't have a lot on, Sarah, do you.'

'Not really, no.'

'Okay. I'd like you to do something for me; it's for an article that's going into the *Pulizija* newsletter.'

'Oh, okay. What is it you want me to do?'

'Research the past careers of Debono, Galea, and Customs Commissioner Prodi. Check how far back they go, any joint investigations; that sort of thing. But first of all, find out what you can about a Corsican called Richard Casanova.'

Said stared at Spiteri. 'And this is for a magazine?'

'Yes... What's wrong with that?'

'Nothing. Okay, I'll get on with it.'

Spiteri ignored Said's reluctance, suspicion even... *I need to know.*

The voicemail light on her phone was flashing again, and Spiteri pressed it without much thought; it couldn't be The Messenger, at least.

Welcome to Voicemail: You have one message.
"I am The Messenger: You have two messages."
Your First Message – "David Naughton."
Your Second Message – "He was where?"

Spiteri stood by her seat, staring at her phone. She was partially taken aback by the message, but she knew something was different. She played the messages again.

'Sarah, come through please. Listen to this.' Spiteri played the messages a third time. 'What do you think?'

'It's not the same voice,' said Said.

'That's what I thought; what else?'

'The messages aren't introduced the same way.'

'Who's David Naughton?'

'Never heard of him; I'll Google it.'

'Use my computer.' Spiteri stood and let Said into her keyboard.

'Actor... Not that well known, I don't think... Biggest film?... *An American Werewolf in London.*'

'Right, let's think. The other messages weren't about the actors; it was a character they played. So Naughton is an American, he's a werewolf... and he's in London at some point,' said Spiteri.

The Maltese Dahlia

'Okay... and that tells us what exactly?' asked Said.

'I don't know, Sarah, but think... what might it mean?'

'The only American that we're dealing with is Wayne.'

'Yes, you're right... Wayne... and what he did to those girls... that could have been the work of a werewolf, right? Poor Daphne thought it was a cannibal after all.'

'In London... Is he saying Wayne is in London?'

'I don't know. Get onto Luqa Airport authorities; get them to check on Wayne flying to London.'

'We already checked that, Inspector.'

'Check again; tell them to go back three months.'

***

'Dad, I want to thank you for this,' said Michael Sammut.

'There's no need. And to be honest I'm not even sure I'm doing the right thing by you,' replied Paul Sammut.

'Why not?'

'Well, your career in the *Pulizija* is over; you know that. And what we are doing inevitably brings us into the world of the Nicola Tizians of this world; are you comfortable with that, you a soon-to-be ex-*Pulizija*?'

'Dad, Malta is a small island, with a lot of small-minded people, but their days are over. A lot of people come here now. This is a business opportunity. We just happen to be the ones who are taking it.'

'Okay, but getting parts locally is one thing. Brought in from abroad is another. We have our first shipment coming in, Michael, and we have nowhere to put it and we haven't even got a deal yet.'

'That's Tizian's problem.'

'Michael, don't be stupid; it is our problem. Tizian is the man in the shadows, always is. Always will be. We knew that. If you weren't happy to agree to that, then you should have said so and we could have walked away.'

***

Dario Grimoldi woke with a start. He had spent another night dozing off and on in his chair in the living room. He had no idea what time he had gotten in. He looked down at his clothes, thought about what he had been wearing the previous night. He was calm. He had on a t-shirt underneath a bathrobe. He knew he must have taken a shower, although he couldn't remember doing it. Grimoldi put his head in his hands. He knew he had failed. He knew if his wife found out, she would want to leave him; just like the first one. *Get dressed, get out, and buy the morning papers; see if there is anything there concerning last night.*

***

Commissioner Kevin Galea stood looking out of his office window; the same window that he had observed Commissioner Debono doing the same on many occasions, and now Debono was dead, and he had taken his place. He remembered a conversation they had had, Debono telling him not to take the job, to retire with him, enjoy his family. But Debono didn't know that he, his partner in crime, hadn't been quite as wise with his benefits as Debono had. Yes, he would be comfortable, but not wealthy.

Galea turned and sat back at his desk. In truth, it wasn't finances that concerned him, it was spiders—or rather, their webs. Years of trade-offs, favours granted, blind eyes turned, had entangled him in a complex web of so-called friends, partners, and associates; just the same as Debono. *And look at him now, Kevin... Look at him now.*

CHAPTER 29

Thea Spiteri's second dinner appointment with Nicola Tizian entranced her more than the first. She called them appointments, as she couldn't contemplate the fact that they might be dates. *It can't happen, Thea. A couple of weeks ago, he was your best friend's partner; and he is still a criminal, no matter how he prefers to describe or explain it. Still...*

Tizian had offered to have her picked up to save her having to drive but Spiteri had insisted on meeting him at a restaurant. Again, the venue that Tizian picked surprised her; another local eatery in a small inland village. Again, the menu was sparse but delicious, the wine equally so, although Spiteri had restricted herself to one glass and no brandy. She found the company and the ambience intoxicating enough.

She hadn't needed an escort home and, once again, Tizian had been a perfect gentleman. Too perfect, perhaps, as Spiteri had been expecting a parting kiss on the cheek and was disappointed that Tizian did not even attempt to oblige.

Spiteri left the restaurant around eleven p.m. and set off for home. Passing by the St Margerita Church, which sits on the Victoria Line—an old, British-built security wall from the war years—at Wied L-Arkata, she noticed what looked like a bundle of clothes lying on the ground.

As she got in line with the dark shape, she detected a movement: someone making an effort to sit up. Spiteri thumped on her brakes and stopped with a screech of tyre on tarmac. Spiteri rushed over to the bundle, helped the waiflike figure sit up, and found herself looking into the cut and bruised face of Laura, the young girl who had identified The Maltese Dahlia as Letizia Corsu.

'You're safe now, Laura. Don't be frightened.' Spiteri lifted the limp body and placed her gently on her backseat. She quickly decided that she was going to take the girl to her house first, clean her up, let her sleep if she wanted. If she had anything wrong that required a doctor, she would call out the doctor on call to the *Pulizija*. Spiteri just had a feeling that Laura's whereabouts be kept quiet for now.

Laura belied her looks; she was a tough individual. An hour after arriving in Spiteri's house, she had had a shower, her abrasions attended to, and was sitting cross-legged on Spiteri's floor, sipping hot chocolate.

'You can stay here till we decide what's best for you, Laura.'

'We decide?'

'Laura, I'm not getting at you. I would like us to become friends, but there is no use you pretending that everything is good in your world. It's obvious it's not.'

Laura hung her head, stared at the mug of chocolate in her hand. 'Did you ever find Christine's killer?'

'Whose killer?'

'Christine's; the papers called her The Maltese Dahlia.'

'That's not the name you gave me, Laura. You told me her name was Letizia Corsu.'

'I know. I thought that was her name; ends up she had a lot of names.'

'How do you know that, Laura?'

'Talk.'

The Maltese Dahlia

Spiteri decided not to press the young girl, who looked more like an elf curled up on her floor than a girl in her teens. *If she is in her teens, that is, Thea.*

'Do you know her real name now?'

'Yes.'

'How do you know this one is her real name?'

'Talk.'

'What is her real name, Laura? Please tell me that.'

Laura looked at a bowl of fruit that was sitting on one of Spiteri's kitchen counters. 'Can I have an apple?'

'Oh God, Laura, I'm sorry. Are you hungry? Do you want me to make you something to eat?'

'Can I have the apple as well?'

Spiteri's heart was breaking. 'Of course. Here. What else would you like?'

'Maybe sandwiches; anything that's easy to carry.'

'Carry, why... Where are you going?'

The elfin-like figure appeared to be in deep thought before she gave a small shrug of her shoulders.

Spiteri sat down on her kitchen floor. 'Laura, I told you: you can stay here as long as you like. I want you to stay. Once I know that you have somewhere safe to go, and how you are going to live, then I will take you there myself. I promise.'

'Are you a lesbo?'

Spiteri's heart broke once more. 'No, Laura... You are safe here.'

'I don't mind if you are. Who cares.' Laura looked around before turning back to Spiteri in a slight panic. 'I don't have any money!'

She had thrown Spiteri. 'Money?'

'Rent money.'

'Laura...' Spiteri couldn't say any more; she felt she was about to cry. She stood up quickly. 'Do you like chicken? Chicken and pasta?'

'With the red sauce, the tomato one?'

Laura's childlike tone cemented Spiteri's determination to find out who had treated her so badly. Spiteri put a pan of water on the cooker and started to chop up some onions; she barely heard the whisper coming from the corner.

'Christine Mangion.'

'What did you say, little one?'

'Christine Mangion; that was Poppins' real name.'

'Are you sure, Laura? I'm not doubting you or anything, but how do you know?'

'Talk.'

'Okay. Thank you for trusting me, Laura.'

'And she wasn't from Sicily.'

'No? Where was she from, do you know?'

'Someplace called Bastia. It's in Corsica. That's an island too, did you know that?'

Spiteri winced as the chopping knife cut into her thumb.

CHAPTER 30

Thea Spiteri didn't sleep well during the night. What Laura had told her the previous night had rocked her but she was more anxious that Laura didn't slip away during the night. Spiteri rose, showered, and dressed as quietly as she could; she wanted Laura to sleep for as long as she needed to, but when she went into the kitchen to make a coffee, Laura was sitting on the floor.

Spiteri's relief at seeing her was almost overwhelming. 'Good morning Laura. Did you sleep okay?'

'The bed smells nice.'

'That's good. Why are you sitting there? Why don't you go through and sit in the living room?'

'My clothes are dirty.'

Spiteri somehow hadn't noticed that Laura was wearing the same clothes that she had on when Spiteri had picked her up. 'Would you like me to wash them?'

'No, it's okay... I don't have any other ones to put on anyway.'

'Laura, I need to go into work this morning, but I'll come and get you this afternoon; we'll go and get you some new clothes. Is that okay with you?'

'Can they be yellow?'

'Yes, if you want... Why yellow?'

Laura shrugged. 'I like yellow.'

'Good answer, little one. Yellow it is, then.'

***

Sarah Said had tried calling Spiteri two or three times through the course of the previous evening without any luck and was on the point of calling her again when Spiteri appeared in the squad room.

'Morning, Sarah.'

'Morning, Inspector. I've been trying to get a hold of you.'

Spiteri looked puzzled at first, but then remembered. Before sitting down to dinner with Nicola Tizian the previous evening, she had switched off her mobile.

'Shit. Sorry, Sarah. I've forgotten to switch my phone back on. Was it important?'

'Very.'

'What is it?'

'John Wayne was in London at the time of the Letizia Corsu killing; a medical conference. I checked with the hotel and the conference organisers. He was definitely there. Not only that, he was there for a week, so even if Paul Sammut was out by a day in his time-of-death estimate, it couldn't have been Wayne.'

Spiteri's thoughts raced to an image of Tizian. *Is this why he's been wining and dining me?*

'You always said it was two different killers, Inspector.'

'Mm, and now we know he's still out there. I'll need to tell the commissioner. Anything else?'

'I researched the guy Casanova you requested me to; he wasn't much like the famous romantic, I'll tell you that.'

'Come through in five minutes and tell me. I want to think about what to do about Wayne and The Dahlia.'

Spiteri slowly sat down at her desk. *That last message, it must be from someone who knew Wayne was in London... and the voice... the voice...*

The Maltese Dahlia

Spiteri rummaged in her bag and took out her phone. She switched back on, saw her missed calls: two from Said and two from Tizian. *Nicola, Nicola... Who are you? What are you?*

Thea Spiteri was unaware as she motioned for Said to sit that her questions were about to be answered.

***

Said placed her notes on the Wayne update on Spiteri's desk. 'Do you want me to leave the Casanova stuff as well or go over it with you?'

'Read it over please, Sarah... Maybe I'll pick up something from hearing it.'

'Right, well... Richard Casanova was a Corsican Mafia boss. Not a Godfather... The Corsican Mafia isn't the same as the Cosa Nostra, apparently. The Corsican Mafia is more like an association of families, no hierarchy as such but fiercely loyal to each other and the other families they are in league with. Each family has a speciality: drugs, prostitution, casinos, whatever... and each family works for the other families in their own speciality. Anyway, Casanova was murdered, surprise surprise, in 2008 and a guy called Germani, Casanova's brother-in-law, took over. He's in prison in France at the moment but still calls the shots; no pun intended.'

'How many families are there?'

'I don't know exactly. I don't think anyone really knows, actually, because there are lots of loose connections that aren't strictly ties. The ones I've seen are Germani, Guazzellis, and Luciani; but like I said, there are quite a few. However, I found out something that you'll really love.'

'What?'

'There's a group of families that, for dim and distant historical reasons, are loyal to Germani. They are called the Venzolasco Bergers Braquers.'

'And?'

'One of the families is the Tizians.'

Spiteri struggled to keep calm. 'And all of this is in your report there?'

'Yes.'

'Okay, thank you, Sarah. Will you go and pull out everything to do with The Dahlia killing? Just The Dahlia, not the other three; Wayne definitely did them, but I want you to start going over everything, from the Swiss girl who found the body up until now. There must be something we're missing. I'm going to call the commissioner now; I'll get help drafted in. Close the door please.'

Spiteri waited till she was alone before letting the tears come. She slammed her fist on Said's report; the pain of the blow brought her to her senses. *No, Thea, you are not doing this. You have been a fool, but you're going to do your job.*

Spiteri lifted the report and Googled Venzolasco Bergers Braquers. It was almost as if a needle had been pressed into her eyes.. There it was... The Tizian family allied to the Germani Gang... no alterations recorded.

Spiteri knew what was next; she scrolled down the page: The Mangra Family"... allied to the Germani Gang, alt: Mangion. *So now we know.*

Spiteri picked up the phone to call Commissioner Galea; she paused, replaced the receiver, and scrolled the page again: The Galiera Family... allied to the Germani Gang, alt: Galea.

One last nail in the coffin, Thea.

There it was: The Debonno Family... allied to the Germani gang... no alterations recorded.

Spiteri slowly rose and walked over to the window. *Dear God, Matt... I miss you so much. Enough; no more victims.*

A spot of make-up, hair brushed back, skirt straightened. Spiteri strolled through the outer office. 'Good work, Sarah. Well done.'

'Did you speak to the commissioner?'

The Maltese Dahlia

'Oh, I think he already knows. I'm out Sarah; I'll not be back in today. I'm going to buy some yellow clothes.'
Said stared nonplussed as the door swung closed.

CHAPTER 31

Thea Spiteri was putting a DVD, the first of the three she had bought Laura, into her player. She turned as Laura walked into the room. 'Very nice, Laura... Very...'

'Banana... ish!'

'That's the word!'

Laura flopped into a bean bag that sat in front of the TV, a KFC Bucket Meal at her side. Spiteri had refused to buy it at first, but when Laura had told her that she'd never had one in her life, she soon relented. *God, what sort of childhood had this waif endured?*

'Laura, like I told you on the way back, I need to go to work for a while, but I won't be late. Maybe we can watch the last DVD together?'

'Okay.'

Spiteri drove towards St Julians knowing that Nicola Tizian would be there but unsure quite what she was going to say. She did know that she would be sending him to prison, though; that was non-negotiable. She got parked near the EC Language School and walked the short distance down into the heart of Paceville—or Tackyville, as the people of Valetta liked to call it.

Spiteri was lucky. Her first guess as to where Tizian might be was right; she strode towards him.

'Ah, Thea, I've been trying to reach you... would you...'

Spiteri walked past Tizian, nodding for him to follow.

'Thea, is something wrong?'

'Wrong? Let me think: a woman is executed. That's what the Dahlia killing was, Nicola, an execution. I've just found out that woman was Corsican, not Sicilian. Her real name was Mangion, a family involved with the Venzolasco Bergers Braquers; but then again, you'd know that, Nicola, wouldn't you, as the Tizian family are linked as well.'

'Thea...'

'Sorry. I forgot to mention she was from Bastia, just like you, and she was working here as a prostitute. Mm, a lot of coincidences there, Nicola, wouldn't you say? So, who might want her dead? Who fits that bill, would you say, Nic? Was she getting greedy, taking a little bit too much for herself?'

'I think you should stop there.'

'Stop? No... I'm just getting to the good bit. Daphne came to me, Nicola. She suspected you, your new business venture... and she ends up dead, too. God, isn't that weird? Yet another coincidence.'

'I thought we had more than that, Thea... or should I say Inspector? Get out.'

'I'm going to nail you, Tizian—and all the others.'

Spiteri rushed back to her car; her eyes full of tears of frustration... or sadness? Not even she knew.

***

Dario Grimoldi had just taken his usual seat on the stairs outside Burger King in Paceville as he saw the forlorn figure of Thea Spiteri rush past him; she appeared to be crying. Grimoldi stared down the road that Spiteri had come from but couldn't see anything unusual. He considered following Spiteri, but just then, a group of girls whose attire left nothing to the imagination walked past and all thought s of Spiteri left Grimoldi's mind.

The Maltese Dahlia

***

I am The Messenger
I do not like to be ignored
I do not like to be restrained
I will always fulfil my destiny.

***

Before she had pulled herself together and decided on her route home, Spiteri found herself going the wrong way and heading down the hill towards St Julians Bay. *Shit, Thea. Pull yourself together.*

A small traffic queue had formed at the corner outside Bill's Bar. Spiteri glanced down to her left and saw the sign for the Crow's Nest, the bar where her lost love Matt had gone to drown his sorrows on occasion. Spiteri contemplated doing the same but knew she had to get back to Laura. She studied the entrance to the bar, willing Matt to walk out, show her that this had all been a bad dream; but instead a small, fair-haired guy wearing a sky blue Adidas t-shirt, came out, walking in that unique way that drunk Glaswegians seem to have made their own, and headed towards the row of cars. He crossed in front of Spiteri's car and, after glancing in, he raised his arms in a victorious boxer pose and shouted "Hey, bone structure!" before heading up the hill singing "One Connie Farooohja, there's only one Connie Faroo... ooo... oh.... ja!" in a broad Scottish accent. Spiteri smiled. *I wonder if he knew Matt? Probably. All the Scots are mad.*

CHAPTER 32

Commissioner Kevin Galea was not like his predecessor, Debono. Whereas Debono had seemed to thrive on the intrigue and deviousness that seemed to go hand in hand with positions of power in Malta, Galea had grown weary of it after only his few months in the post. He couldn't deny, especially to himself, that he had enjoyed some of the "accepted but unrecorded," benefits open to *Pulizija* officers on the way up the career ladder. But the corruption was so blatant now that even an incident where a *Pulizija* officer actually shot at a car in broad daylight, apparently as a security measure; but that was later seen to have murky political intent, was accepted with resignation by the population as just something that they would have to live with. The illness to his daughter; the betrayal of his son-in-law, and the cost of previous alliances was now proving too big a price to pay. The telephone conversation he had just had with Nicola Tizian only underlined the futility of his situation.

***

Galea was unaware that Spiteri was having similar thoughts and that she had reached a completely different conclusion. She was going to tumble the whole deck of cards; and for the first time, she picked up her phone to call Galea, uncertain if she was calling a colleague... or an enemy.

'Commissioner, I need to see you urgently.'

'Yes, I imagine you do. Come over in half an hour.'

Spiteri stared at the phone as she replaced it. Uncertainty filled her mind at Galea's unexpected response. *I'll soon know, I suppose.*

Galea did not keep Spiteri waiting and had her ushered in as soon as she arrived. 'Thea, I am your boss, but I also look upon you as my best officer and a friend. However, that does not mean that you are untouchable. You cannot go around accusing people of murder, prominent people at that, and not expect a backlash.'

'I take it Tizian has been in touch. He's a prominent citizen now?'

'Thea, we may not like him or how he makes a living, but unless we can prove wrongdoing, then he is as innocent as you or I.'

'And how innocent is that, Commissioner?'

'Sorry; what do you mean?'

'I've had to do some background search in relation to the Dahlia killing; it turns out that she is of Corsican extraction.'

'Right... and?'

'So is Tizian.'

'And so, from that, you have deduced that he must have killed her?'

'So was Debono... and so are you.'

Spiteri watched as Galea's expression turned to stone. 'Inspector, be very, very careful before you say any more.'

'Is there more, Kevin? I want to believe there isn't, but I need to know. I am going to get to the bottom of all this.'

'Thea, life is not black and white; there are many shades in between.'

'Shades? Is corruption a shade of justice now?'

'Do you have any proof of corruption?'

The Maltese Dahlia

'No, but if it's there, I will.'

'What do you want, Thea?'

'A twenty-four hour watch on Tizian and the two Sammuts.'

'We've done that, established that they meet and talk. That isn't a crime, either.'

'I need them watched, Commissioner... this time, I'll confront the three of them if they meet.'

'Sorry, no... I need a reason. That's final.'

Spiteri rose and headed as quickly as she could for the door, showing no restraint as she clattered it shut. She knew if she stayed, she would say something that she would regret. As she strode down the corridor, away from Galea's office, she was confused. *Is he being obstructive? Is he in league with Tizian? Has Tizian got something over him? What is Paul Sammut's role in all this?*

Spiteri stopped in her tracks. A conversation with Sammut came back to her. She turned and almost ran back to Galea's office. She pushed through the door without even glancing at the commissioner's secretary. 'Drugs!'

Galea was taken aback at first by the intrusion, but quickly gathered himself together.

'What about drugs?'

'Kevin, when I spoke to Paul Sammut about the Dahlia post-mortem, he told me he hadn't done a rectal temperature check.'

'So?'

'So where is a common place for drug mules to hide drugs? How would an angry drug lord look for drugs in someone they thought was swallowing some of his shipment? He'd cut her open, that's how. I want the body disinterred and another PM done, but not by Paul Sammut.'

Galea sat thinking for a few moments. 'Okay, I'll get that organised. I'll call you when it's been approved.'

Spiteri turned and headed back towards the door; she felt one hundred percent more positive this time than she had a few minutes earlier.

'Oh, Inspector...'

Spiteri turned, looked at Galea.

'Paul Sammut isn't Corsican. Please close the door quietly this time.'

***

After he had finished talking to Galea, Nicola Tizian had called Paul Sammut and arranged a meeting with him and Michael at the Fort Coffee Shop in Birgu.

'We might need to change our supply chain,' said Tizian.

'Why?' asked Michael Sammut.

'Our supplier is starting to get cold feet. He feels some of the shipments we're talking about are too large.'

'Too large? What's he talking about? How can they be too large?'

'He means the monies involved, not the items.'

'Well, we'll just have to use other suppliers, then.'

'That's easier said than done, Michael. We told him the stuff has to be high quality, able to be traced to source. Not everyone will do that.'

'How are things with you and the minister; are they going to turn a blind eye? What cut do they want?'

Tizian looked at his new business partners. All his doubts about this venture wouldn't go away. On the other hand, they would be easy to push aside if the time came.

Spiteri, on the other hand, was an obstacle he hadn't suspected; but she, too, could be pushed aside if needs be. Tizian surprised himself by feeling a little depressed at that possibility.

***

The Maltese Dahlia

Sarah Said had just gotten up to go for lunch when her phone went.

'Sarah, it's me. The Dahlia file; you have everything, yes?' said Spiteri.

'Yes, I have it here.'

'Good. Listen, concentrate on the PM Report. I want you to go through it sentence by sentence. Let me know if anything, anything, seems different to a normal PM. I know the body was in two pieces and had had organs removed, but I don't mean that. I want anything that Sammut has put in the report, or left out of the report, that is different from normal. Is that clear?'

'Yes.'

'I've asked Galea to organise the paperwork to get The Dahlia exhumed. Now listen, Sarah, not a word to anyone about that; Paul Sammut won't be doing the second PM.'

'I wouldn't say anything.'

'I know, Sarah. I'm not doubting you; I'm just unsure about who we can and cannot trust. I'll see you in the morning.'

Spiteri threw her mobile onto the passenger seat and headed off to pick up Laura. She felt a growing bond forming with the girl, who had been dealt a hand even worse than Spiteri herself. People had helped Spiteri, and now Spiteri was going to pass that forward. She smiled as she recalled Laura's face that morning, when she had said that she would take her to lunch that afternoon. 'We'll go to a Chinese...' Spiteri thought Laura was going to burst, her excitement was so palpable. At the same time, Spiteri knew that it would soon be time to talk about Laura's future. That was going to be a difficult task, as Laura always retreated into herself whenever the conversation turned to her life: past, present, or future.

CHAPTER 33

As it was such a beautiful morning, Sarah Said had decided to walk into work. The sun's rays, and the sea breeze blowing in from the Grand Harbour area of Valetta, helped to raise her spirits even if her thoughts kept returning to Michael Sammut. Said had learned from previous times that you cannot be one hundred percent sure of even a colleague's real thoughts and intentions; but she still found it difficult to accept that Sammut was involved in illegal activities, even if the evidence would seem to indicate otherwise. She arrived in the office before anyone else and switched on the lights, coffee percolator, and her PC before catching a glimpse of her reflection in an office window. Said did not consider herself to be beautiful; she awarded herself passable on a good day. *You're getting old, Sarah... and grumpy... and maybe even a bit paranoid... and...*

A desk phone rang and pulled her out of her self-analysis. 'Sergeant Said.'

'Ah, good morning, Sergeant. It's Commissioner Galea. Is Inspector Spiteri in yet?'

'No, I'm sorry. She's not.'

'That's okay, can you let her know that since it seems that The Dahlia victim has no family or friends, the permissions for the disinterment have been granted quicker than usual, so it is going ahead tomorrow morning. Dr Samaras will fly in at seven a.m. I've arranged for him to be picked up at Luqa; everything should be concluded by midday.'

'Yes, Commissioner, I'll let her know, thank you. Oh, incidentally, I'm nearly finished the research for the magazine article.'

'The magazine article?'

'Yes, the one for the *Pulizija* Journal... the one about commissioners past and present, different departments, et cetera.'

Said was unsure for a moment over whether she had been cut off. 'Oh, yes... That article. Good, very good. Good-bye, Sergeant.' Galea slowly hung up his phone. *So, it seems as if Inspector Spiteri is on a crusade... very apt for Malta, I suppose.*

***

Nicola Tizian was troubled, not by any of the issues that normally troubled him but by the feeling of disappointment that he was feeling over Spiteri. The accusations she was making against him were one thing—those he could handle—but the feeling of loss was another. He knew he wasn't in love with Spiteri, as he had never been in love with any woman, not even Daphne Arrigo; but there was something inside of him that had been aroused by being in Spiteri's company. Maybe it was the thrill of fraternising with the enemy, maybe it was the challenge of getting Spiteri to see the world from a different angle... maybe it was lust. Tizian didn't have any answers, but he had the feelings—and Nicola Tizian always believed that feelings needed to be acted upon.

***

After being updated by Said on her arrival at work, Thea Spiteri sat at her desk pondering her next move. She was glad that the second PM was going ahead the next day and that Galea hadn't stalled on moving things on. *Maybe you're wrong about him, Thea.*

Laura had still been sleeping when Spiteri left for work an hour previously, but she was looking forward to going home that evening, as Laura had insisted that she was going to cook dinner. They had laughed together as Spiteri tried to guess what Laura would make, but Laura had insisted it was to be a surprise. It would be.

***

I am The Messenger
I deliver pain
I deliver sorrow
I will not be discarded

***

A call from Nicola Tizian also had Paul Sammut and Michael Sammut considering their next moves. Michael, despite his enthusiasm for the news, had always had his conscience troubling him about his *Pulizija* connection. Then and there, he made the decision to resign. Paul Sammut, on the other hand, felt that his future was being settled by others. Although he had no moral dilemma over Tizian's news, he was perturbed by Tizian's closing comments. 'Why are you doing a second PM on The Dahlia?'

'I'm not.'

'Well, somebody is. I hope you didn't miss anything, Paul.'

'What makes you think there's going to be a second PM?'

'Spiteri was in here the other day accusing me of; well, I'm not sure of what exactly, but it was to do with The Dahlia.'

'That doesn't mean a second PM has been ordered.'

'No... why else exhume the body, then?'

Paul Vincent Lee

***

Thea Spiteri was worried that people would think she was mad as she wandered around the supermarket with a huge smile on her face, buying up foods she knew she could cook quickly. She didn't doubt Laura's sincerity, just her ability.

CHAPTER 34

The following morning, Spiteri was sitting at her desk, waiting for a phone call from Dr Samaras. She would have described her mood as "anxious anticipation" if anyone asked. No one did, so Spiteri could tell the truth to herself: She was devastated. There had been no evening meal with Laura the previous night, cooked by Laura or otherwise. Spiteri had guessed there was something wrong as soon as she had entered the house; it was too normal. Normal, as before Laura came. No TV on; no mess on the living room floor from DVD cases... no life. Spiteri had immediately checked Laura's room. Neat, tidy... and empty. She searched the house for signs of a struggle... nothing. She searched for a note... nothing. The only thing out of place was Spiteri's photo album. She picked it up to put back on the shelf. She looked at the pages on show... nothing. A few pictures of squad nights out; a birthday dinner for Sarah, a Welcoming New Colleagues pizza night... nothing. The picture of her, Said, Grimoldi, and Michael Sammut, all with raised glasses was one that Spiteri had liked at the time: *What an illusion pictures can be.* Spiteri was tempted to flick through the book but she knew there were pictures of her with Daphne, with Matt... with Tizian... she couldn't face that.

Her phone rang. 'Spiteri.'

'Inspector, it is Dr Samaras.'

'Yes, Doctor, have you found any discrepancies?'

'Not discrepancies as such, no… but I must congratulate you, Inspector, on your intuition. A condom, containing what is undoubtedly heroin, was lodged in the victim's anus. In fact, it was implanted there, held in by gauze and two sutures.'

'Cause of death?'

'Dr Sammut's finding was correct; blows to the head.'

'Thank you, Doctor.'

Spiteri hung up, unsure whether to be pleased or upset; it could have been a genuine mistake on Paul Sammut's part, or he was in league with Tizian. *But why not remove the drugs in that case? Perhaps Tizian had told him they were in her stomach? Maybe these drugs were The Dahlia's little secret? A secret that got her killed.*

Spiteri felt she had the upper hand now; she couldn't waste time. 'Commissioner Galea. Please let him know it's urgent.'

'Inspector.'

'The Dahlia's body had drugs hidden inside it.'

'I know. Dr Samaras reports to me, Inspector.'

Spiteri paused, unsure how to proceed. 'I want the surveillance reinstated on the Sammuts, Commissioner.' She had a follow-up line ready but was praying she wouldn't have to use it. She waited for Galea's response.

'I'll authorise that now.'

'Tizian too.'

'No. There is nothing connecting him to this situation.'

'Nothing connecting him… are you serious?'

'Perfectly, you have no…'

'I'm sure *The Malta Times* will be interested in your views, Commissioner.'

'You have just made a career-changing decision, Inspector.' And with that, the line went dead.

'Fuck.'

The Maltese Dahlia

***

The new stretch of coast road being built on the east coast of Malta, from The Water Park to St Paul's Bay, was a gift from heaven for Chris Palmier. Chris was a young man who had concentrated on football and girls when he was at school and now found it extremely difficult to get work. But he was strong, fit, and healthy and wasn't afraid of manual labour. He had impressed his bosses with his commitment, and they had discussed keeping him on when their contract on the road works ended. Therefore, his manager was surprised when he turned up on site to see Palmier sitting down on a rock. As he walked over to Palmier, his manager was hit by a terrible odour. This wasn't unusual on this site, as it was right beside the old rubbish dump for the island, but this smell was particularly bad. 'Chris, what's...'

Palmier's outstretched finger pointing to one of the drainage ditches cut off the rest of his manager's sentence. Palmier's boss took a few steps past his traumatised employee. 'I'll call the *Pulizija*. Go and sit in one of the cabins, Chris.'

The single lane traffic moving at a snail's pace along the route caused Spiteri and Said to take an hour to get to the site from Floriana. There were already several *Pulizija* on the scene when Spiteri joined them. 'We're just waiting for the pathologist, Inspector. Not that we really need confirmation of death. Then we'll check for I.D.'

'No need... His name is Peter Abela; he was the chief executive at Mater Dei Hospital.'

At that point, a car drew up and Paul Sammut emerged. He walked over to the group containing Spiteri was standing. He didn't acknowledge or even look in her direction. 'Oh good. A body I am allowed to look at.' Everyone in the group, except Spiteri, was slightly bemused, even more so when he added, 'My last case, gentlemen. If I actually do the PM, that is!' Spiteri was already walking away but heard every word.

She hardly spoke on the journey back to the office. *Had he jumped or was he pushed? Is Galea keeping Paul Sammut informed?*

Spiteri dashed straight into her office and called Galea again. 'Has Paul Sammut resigned?'

'Yes, and his son, Michael. You do go through an incredible amount of officers, Inspector. I think that will have to be looked at; maybe have you reassigned to less stressful duties.'

She ignored the inference. 'What reason did he give... they give?'

'Paul Sammut said that it was obvious that the *Pulizija* department had lost faith in him. Michael didn't give a reason. I don't suppose he needs to; it's rather obvious, I would say.'

'Really? Well, it's not obvious to me.'

'Inspector, that is now two Detective Sergeants and one Detective Constable you have gone through in a year. How much more obvious does it need to be?'

'That is so unfair. You yourself have said on many occasions that I was your best officer, but now that I've touched your fucking Corsican nerve, you are out to get me. Fine, we shall see how it goes, but I can assure you, if I am hindered in my investigations in any way, I'll go to the Minister and the papers... the bloody Vatican if I have to...' The click on the phone showed Spiteri that the conversation was over.

She didn't realise then that all the investigations, and a chapter of her life, would soon be over, too.

CHAPTER 35

A feeling of desperate loneliness overwhelmed Spiteri as she sat in her kitchen, reluctantly picking at a tuna salad. Laura had only been at the house a few nights, but had left an indelible mark. Spiteri knew she could search for her, on her own if not officially, but knew there would be no point. Laura did not want to be there.

With a pang of guilt, Spiteri had earlier checked where she kept a small amount of money and some credit cards. She checked her jewellery box and made a cursory check of CDs and DVDs... nothing had been taken. She held her breath as she opened the wardrobe in Laura's room. The clothes Spiteri had bought Laura were gone. Spiteri was glad: They were a present, not a bribe.

Spiteri moved over to her wine rack and pulled out a bottle of Shiraz. She uncorked it, selected a glass, and wandered into her living room. 'Well couch, looks like it's back to me and you.' She flopped onto the couch and poured a glass of the velvet liquid, but before she could take her first sip, her mobile rang. She was tempted to ignore it. *It might be Laura.*

She grabbed the phone without looking at the screen. 'Laura?'

'Sorry, Thea, it's Pietro Cassar.'

'It's okay, Pietro; I was asking more in hope than expectation. What's up?'

'No, nothing, but I can't get a hold of Galea, so I thought I'd better call you.'

'What is it?'

'Well, Tizian and both the Sammuts have just sat down to dinner in Da Pippo; do you know it?'

'Yes, and it's perfect. Not many people know this, but there is a rear entrance from the lane leading to the park. I'll use that; surprise them.'

'Eh, are you intending on arresting them? You can't do that on your own, especially with Tizian involved.'

'No, I just want to let them know that they're being watched. It might disrupt their drug business. Sho knows.'

'Okay. I'll stick around till you arrive.'

'Okay, thanks. One thing, though, why were you calling Galea anyway? This is my initiative.'

'Galea insisted that all developments had to be reported to him first.'

A few moments passed before Spiteri replied, 'Oh, yea, that's right... I forgot.'

As she sped to Da Pippo, Spiteri's anger at Galea's obvious manipulation only made her all the more determined to finish this operation once and for all. She arrived half an hour later, acknowledged Cassar on the radio, walked down the rear side lane, and entered the restaurant.

Spiteri couldn't tell if it was good luck or bad luck, but as she entered the corridor, she saw Nicola Tizian standing with his back to her, deep in conversation on his mobile. She quietly approached.

'Do you have it?' said Tizian.

Spiteri couldn't hear the response, but it pleased Tizian.

'Good, I'll let my clients know... I'll get back to you, tell you how it's to be brought in.'

The Maltese Dahlia

Tizian finished his call and walked back to the dinner table, not really noticing the look of surprise on the Sammuts' faces.

'Your clients, Nicola? That will be the Sammuts here, I suppose.'

'Thea, how lovely to see you; I was going to call you, see if you had come to your senses. Please take a seat.'

Spiteri ignored Tizian and looked at the Sammuts. 'I thought at first it was body parts you were all getting excited about; but no, it's heroin.'

'Drugs? Body parts? What in God's name are you talking about, woman?' roared Paul Sammut.

'We did a second PM on The Dahlia today; lo and behold, she was a drug courier.'

'We know all about that. As it happens, I've resigned anyway, and so has Michael. I made a mistake, I've apologised to Galea, and I'll apologise to you now, but it was a genuine mistake.'

'Right, so let me tell you my version of that story. Mr Tizian here, a member of the Corsican Mafia who makes his living in Malta on the back of prostitution, amongst other things, hires a girl from his hometown. She does a bit of exotic dancing then is offered more lucrative work, bringing in heroin. Problem is, she sees it's so lucrative that she decides to keep some for herself. Except she makes a mistake; she talks a little bit too loudly. Mr Tizian here isn't pleased. Voila, one dead Corsican girl. And that's not all; this has been an ongoing business built up over many years. He couldn't do it alone; he needed allies, disappearing evidence. Enter Paul Sammut... Who is going to question his PM Reports? No one. Next, it would be great to have someone in the *Pulizija* to keep him informed about any investigations. Boom, enter Michael Sammut, Detective Constable and son of the aforementioned Paul Sammut.'

Da Pippo was busy, and there was an affable atmosphere from the various groups enjoying their meals, but the silence from Tizian's table appeared to almost drown it out. Finally, Tizian spoke. 'Inspector, please sit. Listen to what I, we, have to say; then I promise on Daphne's life that I will answer any questions you have.'

Spiteri's immediate reaction was to ignore Tizian and finish with a promise that she was going to nail them all, but something in the expressions of the three men looking at her made her change her mind. She sat down. Tizian had poured her a glass of wine before she had even noticed.

'Who would like to begin?' asked Tizian.

To Spiteri's surprise, Michael Sammut offered.

'Inspector Spiteri, you were aware that I wasn't particularly fulfilled in the *Pulizija*; it is a great job, worthwhile, but it just wasn't for me. You also knew that things were strained with my father; I felt that I had let him down, and I also couldn't understand why it was that my parents were so against me becoming an actor or scriptwriter, or even have a passion for movies. It was a case of doctor or scrapheap. Dad...'

Paul Sammut took over. 'Michael has just used the important word: passion. I had been too blind to see that my attitude was making my own son miserable, that I was forcing him away from me. I was distraught at my stupidity. Thea, you may or may not be aware that the Maltese government sees the film industry as one of the future mainstays of its economy, and they are putting heavy financial backing behind those beliefs. The industry is responding; you'll know I'm sure that *Gladiator*, *Troy*, and many other films have been shot here. I went to Michael basically to say how sorry I was for causing him pain, but in the course of our conversation, Michael told me of this business dream he had. He wanted to ride on the back of Malta's enthusiasm for the film industry and its reliance on the tourist trade and open a theme park based on the movies. And not just a small tacky park; an all-year-round tourist attraction, world class... maybe not quite Disney standard to start, but who knows? I loved the idea and wanted to give my son my full support, and although I am not poor, I don't have the sums of money or the contacts that it would take to make something like this work—and, let's be honest, the political influence. I thought about who on the island might fit that bill and came up with Nicola.'

Spiteri was almost lost for words, her mind racing. 'Political influence?'

'This is a huge enterprise and will require the acquisition, or lease, of a large swath of land... which, as you know, is a very touchy, almost touching on morality, issue here.'

Michael Sammut interrupted. 'The other issue is what we want to put in the park. We want authentic movie memorabilia; we want film studios to see us as a marketing opportunity... They scratch our backs, we scratch theirs; a win-win situation. For example, last month I paid a month's salary to buy the knife Richard Widmark used in the film *The Alamo* when he played Jim Bowie, famous for the Bowie knife.'

'Michael, why didn't you talk to me about this?' asked Spiteri.

'Inspector, you had murders to think about; I didn't think the daydreams of a rookie DC would be of much interest.'

'I suppose you're right. But can I give you one piece of advice, a final command, if you like?'

'What?'

'Go and speak to Sarah; she deserves that.'

Michael Sammut looked awkward. 'I've wanted to, but I don't know what to say.'

'Just speak with the passion you have shown tonight.'

'I'll drive you, son.'

The Sammuts took their leave and Spiteri turned to Tizian. 'The Sammuts may be innocent, but you aren't; this changes nothing.'

***

The following morning, Spiteri called a beaming Said into her office. 'And bring me a coffee; you owe me that at least!'

A few minutes later, Said appeared with a coffee... and croissant with strawberry jam.

'Bribery is corruption you know, Sergeant,' teased Spiteri. 'Spare me the details, but how are you and Michael?'

'He called last night, asked me to come over to his house. I was reluctant at first, and then he told me it was a direct order from you!'

'A slight misrepresentation, but go on.'

'I went over, Michael ushered me into the living room, and his parents were sitting there. I was a bit nonplussed for a second and then Paul Sammut explained everything. I think Michael's mother is still lukewarm to the whole thing, but...'

'What do you think of his idea?'

'I think it's great, I really do; I just wish Tizian wasn't involved.'

'Same. Sarah, I need to know now. Not later. Now... I'm going after Tizian. If I get him, it probably means the end of Michael's dream. Do you want a transfer? I can't afford conflict of interest.'

'No.'

'You're sure?'

'Yes.'

'Right; here's the situation as I see it: the body parts theory, as a business, is out. Wayne killed the three girls for his own ends. The Dahlia was killed by someone else, probably Tizian and probably because she was skimming some of his drugs. Paul Sammut made a genuine mistake in the first PM. That, in a way, is good; simplifies things. We can concentrate on Tizian, drugs, and prostitution.'

Spiteri's phone rang. 'Commissioner.'

'I hear your confrontation went well.'

Spiteri tried to turn the tide. 'Yes, very, thanks. We can concentrate on the one person now.'

'In that case, may I offer you a bit of advice?'

'Of course.'

'Check the visitor's book at Carradino.'

Spiteri was lost in thought for a moment. 'What do you mean, Commissioner? The names of who visited Debono?'

'Perhaps, perhaps not.' And with that, the line went dead.

'Sarah, contact Carradino. Get a list of the names of everyone that visited Debono. In fact, go there, get the book; I don't trust anyone involved in this mess. I'm going out. I'll be back before you though. I'll wait for you here.'

CHAPTER 36

Thea Spiteri knew from her conversations with Daphne Arrigo that Nicola Tizian liked to be in his club for ten a.m. to check the previous day's business receipts. The guard outside the door appeared uncertain whether to stop Spiteri as she marched towards the door; but fortunately for him, the office door opened. Nicola Tizian glanced at the guard and then Spiteri. 'Can you bring coffee, Franco... Two cups. Good morning, Inspector, please come in. Take a seat.'

Spiteri spoke before she sat. 'How did you know who Wayne was?'

'Pardon?'

'How did you know to go after Wayne for Daphne's murder?'

'I'd met him before.'

'How? When?'

'He had approached Debono with a business proposition; Debono wanted to see if I would be interested.'

'And were you?'

'No. The man was an uncultured moron, doctor or no doctor.'

'What was the business proposal?'

Tizian smiled. 'He, too, wanted to open some sort of movie theme park. Paul Sammut had already approached me—to be honest, I was sceptical at first—but after I found out Wayne was thinking along the same lines, I looked into it more. It could be very lucrative for the island, Thea.'

'And you.'

'Making money is not a crime.'

'That still doesn't explain how you linked Daphne with Wayne; it could have been any doctor at Mater Dei.'

'Abela told me.'

'Abela!'

'Yes.'

'You never told me you had spoken to Abela.'

'You never asked. Look, Thea, you're right; it could have been anyone Daphne was using, but I called Abela. He told me he had recruited the contact from USA, I asked him how many American doctors he'd recruited, he told me one… and like I said, I'd already met Wayne, the poor man's Texas Ranger.'

Spiteri rose to leave. 'Did you visit Debono in prison?'

'No.'

'Are you sure?'

Tizian stared at Spiteri with his face-of-granite stare. 'Inspector, you may not like me now. That is unfortunate, but do not insult me. Please leave.'

***

I am The Messenger
I have had setbacks
I have had regrets
I have never had failure.

***

As she had guessed, Spiteri had arrived back in her office before Said. Whilst waiting for Said's return, she had two trains of thought running through her head. *What did Galea mean by "perhaps?" Either a name is on a list, or it is not… Did Nicola Tizian kill The Dahlia, Abela, and Wayne, or is he completely innocent of any connection to the crimes?*

Spiteri twitched when she realised her phone was ringing. 'Spiteri.'

'Inspector, I'm sorry to bother you. My name is Sergeant Mifsud; I work in Vice. We arrested a man in the early hours this morning. We've been watching him for a while but didn't know who he was; only that the girls knew him as "The Saviour." We arrested him bundling one of the working girls into a van; he had knocked her around a bit.'

'Okay, but why are you telling me about this?' Spiteri's hand shook as she asked, thoughts of Laura filling her head.

'He says he'll only speak to you.'

'What's his name?'

'Dario Grimoldi.'

'What is the girl's name?' *Please God, no.*

'Alexis. She's Russian.'

'Can you have him brought to Floriana? I can't leave the office at the moment.'

'Yes, of course.'

Spiteri had only replaced the receiver a few moments when it rang again.

'Inspector, it's Paul Sammut. I have my report on the Peter Abela killing.'

'Paul, listen. I'm sorry about my accusations, but...'

'No need; you were only doing what you had to do. Michael understands that, too.'

'Thank you, Paul. So, Abela?'

'Simple enough. Cause of death: bullet wound to side of the head.'

'How long ago?'

'Hard to say for sure, but I'd say right around the time he and Wayne went missing.'

'Right, so about a fortnight ago?'

'Yes, give or take a day.'

'Okay, thanks, Paul.'

Something felt wrong to Spiteri. She opened her notes on Abela and picked up her phone. 'Put me through to Fraud please. Hi, this is Inspector Spiteri; you are investigating missing funds from Mater Dei?'

'Yea, the chief exec is lying on a beach in the Bahamas, we think.'

'Well, actually he's lying in the mortuary at Mater Dei, and before he was lying there, he was lying near a beach certainly; but under the new coast road.'

'Shit.'

'What date did the funds get transferred?'

'Let me just bring it up on the screen: Okay, let's see... Right, the money disappeared ten days ago.'

'Right, well unless it was done through a medium, it wasn't Abela.'

'Shit.'

How eloquent the fraud officers are. Spiteri glanced up and saw Said coming in with the prison visiting book. 'I'll leave you to it, then. Bye.' She fingered through the pages referring to Debono's visitors: *A lot less than I thought; people are distancing themselves.* But after studying the names for nearly half an hour, Spiteri was none the wiser as to what she was supposed to be seeing.

'Right, Sarah, let's grab some lunch and we'll get back to these names after we question the prisoner.'

'Prisoner?'

'Yes, didn't I mention that?'

'No.'

'Oh, sorry; yes, Dario Grimoldi is on his way in under escort. Pizza?'

CHAPTER 37

Dario Grimoldi looked a shadow of the man who had been one of Spiteri's colleagues only a short time before. Despite that, he didn't look overly concerned to be sitting on the opposite side of an interrogation table as the one he was used to.

'Thank you for coming to clear this up, Inspector.'

'Well, can we just deal with what has been going on first, Dario?'

Grimoldi smiled. 'I see you got my message; you were very quick. Well done.'

'What are you talking about?'

'Surely you must have guessed by now that it was me who led you to John Wayne Gacy; and quite cleverly at that, even though I say so myself.'

'That message was from you? How did you know about Wayne?'

'When I saw the news coverage, something triggered in my head. Then I remembered the dates didn't match. I'd studied The Dahlia files, remember?'

'Okay, well thank you for that, Dario. I still need to know what your situation now is.'

'Simple. I left the *Pulizija* because I felt I could do more for society. I've spent my time talking to the girls, the Maltese girls, who are putting themselves in such danger in Paceville; I show them there is another way.'

'You talk to the girls; that's all?'

'Yes, of course. They call me The Saviour... It was a joke at first, but I like it.'

'My colleagues in the vice squad say there have been complaints about you; they say you have beaten some of the girls.' The words had no sooner left Spiteri's mouth than she froze. Memories of the night she rescued Laura spun around in her head.

'That's rubbish. Yes, some of the girls; the drugs have such a pull on them that they try to run away. I need to restrain them sometimes.'

'Restrain them?'

Grimoldi stayed silent.

'Wait here.' Spiteri went to the rest room, where the sergeant from vice was talking to Said. 'Sergeant, Dario Grimoldi, do you have a record of what girls complained about him?'

'We have a record of sorts; the girls don't really want to speak to us. They usually don't give their real names.'

'Do you have their pictures?'

'Not officially, but I have some on my phone.'

'Can I see?'

'Sure.' The sergeant flicked through the grainy images. 'Sorry. I know the quality isn't great, but they're taken under difficult circumstances.'

'Stop! Go back one.' An unmistakeable image of Grimoldi and Laura walking away from Paceville was frozen in time. 'When was this picture taken?' Sergeant Mifsud pressed a button; a date and time registered over the photo.

'Thank you, Sergeant. I think I may love you. Sarah, come with me.'

On the way back to the interview room, all Spiteri could think about was her photo album: *Poor Laura, looking through the book, sees me with her tormentor, Grimoldi... his arm over my shoulder... She takes off.*

The Maltese Dahlia

Spiteri and Said walked back into the interview room. 'Hi, Sarah,' said Grimoldi. 'So is everything sorted out, Inspector?'

'Yes. You're under arrest.'

***

'I feel a bit sorry for him,' said Said as she sat down opposite Spiteri to go over the prison visitors book.

'He was beating up vulnerable young girls, Sarah.'

'I know. I'm not defending him, but he's clearly slightly gone in the head.'

'Well, that's for others to decide. Right, the people who visited Debono; any ideas?'

'Not really; I thought about it on the way back from Carradino and during lunch. I don't see any of them killing Debono.'

'No, either do I. Why did Galea bring it up, then, and what does "perhaps" mean? I'll need to call him, make myself look even more incompetent.'

There would be no need; Commissioner Galea was on the line.

'Good afternoon, Commissioner.'

'You have the book?'

'What book is that, Commissioner?'

'Don't be flippant, Thea. It demeans both of us.'

Spiteri was chastised. *Rightly so, you stupid woman.* 'Sorry, Commissioner; yes, I have it.'

'And... any thoughts?'

'None that I can repeat in polite company.'

'Ha, never mind, restraint is good for the soul. Be in my office at nine a.m. tomorrow, Inspector.'

Spiteri started doodling on the outside of a file that was lying on her desk. *Quicker than I thought. He probably wants it done quickly; get a new inspector in place, then allocate the new team to work under them.*

Spiteri walked over to the bookcase, considered getting her brandy out but resisted. Instead, she ran her fingers along the line of books that had accumulated there over the years; the one on top of a bundle at the end of a shelf caught her eye: *For Whom the Bell Tolls*. Spiteri smiled, turned, picked up her bag and walked out of her office. She never looked back. *We'll see what tomorrow brings.*

***

Nicola Tizian had thought long and hard before calling Galea. He had lived by the view that when you are in complicated situations, make your story as close to the truth as possible; only tampering slightly with it to suit your purposes. Some of Galea's responses to his call had surprised him, saddened him even; but they had finally agreed the best course of action.

Nicola Tizian strolled out of his office and into the warm evening air. He never looked back. *We'll see what tomorrow brings.*

CHAPTER 38

Thea Spiteri sat in an ornate chair in the hallway outside Commissioner Kevin Galea's office. She looked over at Galea's personal secretary, who had been at her desk when Spiteri arrived although Spiteri had made a point of being in plenty of time. Spiteri wasn't sure if she was being paranoid or intuitive but she was aware of the secretary not making eye contact or engaging in any form of small talk. *The loneliness of the condemned prisoner, Thea.*

In truth, in wasn't loneliness that Spiteri felt, but a mixture of sadness and anger. *I have worked so hard to get here, made so many sacrifices... for what? Cast adrift because I wanted to do my job properly.* Spiteri knew that she wouldn't be demoted; they had no case for that and she had done nothing wrong. She would be re-allocated. Given a glorious career development opportunity: Thea... you are now Inspector in Charge of Traffic Cones on Comino. *Well, fuck all of you; I will not be going quietly.*

The telephone on the secretary's desk buzzed. 'You can go in now, Inspector Spiteri.' *Was that a smile or a scowl?* Spiteri rose, tapped on the commissioner's door gently, and entered.

***

Jeddah Airport was a haven from the blistering heat outside. He felt everything had gone well. Yes, he had been surprised when he got the call, maybe even a little apprehensive at first, but an apology, the offer of a private jet, and figures in the millions being bandied about convinced John Wayne that the Gold Rush was about to begin. He hadn't been surprised that the king himself had not been at any of the meetings; he realised that he had to adapt to their way of doing business, and not the other way around. Some of the questions they asked didn't seem relevant to him; but he was glad he had taken the initiative: Bruce Willis, *Die Hard 2*.

He glanced up at the departures screen; his flight to Heathrow left in an hour. He was annoyed, and a bit frazzled, that he had had to bring three suitcases with him, but he was determined: *I ain't leaving anything behind in that shit-hole Malta. Where's my gate?*

'Excuse me sir, are you travelling First Class to Heathrow, London?'

'Why yes, yes I am.'

'No mystery, sir. I saw the tags on your bag; let me help you. First Class on Saudi Airways has a separate check-in. This way please.'

***

Heathrow Airport was as busy as he had ever seen it. He was pleased about that; anonymity all the easier to achieve. Busy or not, he wasn't really affected. First Class Travel to Washington DC had its advantages even before you boarded your flight as well as when you were on board. The separate departure lounge was one of them. He studied a menu and contemplated what meal he would have to celebrate his new venture.

***

The Maltese Dahlia

Thea Spiteri was confused as she sat down in front of the commissioner. She felt like she had been watching a film and two important scenes had been cut out. Galea seemed almost jovial, certainly not like an executioner about to deliver the coup de grace.

'Thea, have you had breakfast? I have ordered one of anything I thought you might like! I'll pour you a coffee while you decide.'

Spiteri's gaze moved from Galea to the plates containing rolls, croissants, cold meat... and back to Galea. The puzzlement on her face must have alerted him.

'I know, Thea, this is not what you were expecting; but take your coffee and anything else you want; we are going to have a long talk.'

Spiteri still hadn't uttered a word since she had entered the room; she stayed that way and waited for Galea to continue.

'Thea, I have often said, to you and others, that you are my best officer; and that is true. In that case, I know you are wondering about whether I am, in some way, involved with what people, laughingly, refer to as the Corsican Mafia.

'My answer to that question has to be yes; but Thea, there is no Corsican Mafia. Confused? Let me explain. The Corsican Mafia is just a convenient name for an alliance of families. It...'

Spiteri interrupted. 'Commissioner, I know all this. We...'

It was Galea's turn to interrupt. 'Yes, but what you don't know is that people who are not involved in their activities, but who are still tied by blood and tradition, cannot, and will not, take positive action against those who do.'

'So what are you saying is that you know of criminal activity but you don't do anything about it, even though you are head of the *Pulizija*!'

'Listen to my words, Thea. I will not take positive action, no; but I will not obstruct those who do. Do you understand my point?'

'I understand it, although I cannot agree with it. Basically, you are saying you are bound by a kind of omerta; something similar to the Sicilian Mafia code of silence?'

'If you like. Thea, you have to understand, there are examples all over the world. In the history of people moving from their homelands, searching for a better life, they stick together, look out for each other.'

'There can't be one law for one and not another.'

'Tell that to any minority in a foreign land. Look, when you are young and headstrong, you think it is okay, letting friends off with certain things, taking a few presents at Christmas, a couple of free drinks in the bars. Later on, you see that it is wrong, and you draw back from it. But some can't give up, they are addicted to the power; Debono is a good example.'

'And you, Commissioner... could you give up?'

'Yes, I was never that involved anyway, but I am still guilty in a way, as I allowed my responsibilities as a Corsican to outweigh my responsibilities as *Pulizija* on occasions. I say "in a way" because my way of meeting all my obligations was to light the way so others, like you, could walk the path.'

'Give me examples.'

'I told you to visit Debono, but I went before you, told him his choices.'

'Your name wasn't in the visitors book.'

'I was there, along with Customs Commissioner Prodi.'

'He's not in the book either.'

'No, and who was it that told you to examine the book?'

'But I still don't understand why.'

'What name is on that list; who is not a visitor?'

'No one's.'

The Maltese Dahlia

'Think again.'

'We checked; all the people visited.'

'No, Thea, not all.'

Spiteri's frustration was starting to show. 'Look, there were only half a dozen names. Governor Scicluna signed it off. I've read...'

'Check the governor's name on your Corsican name source.'

'You're not saying that Governor Scicluna killed Debono?'

'No.'

'What were you both doing there?'

'Reminding Debono of his responsibilities.'

'What was his reaction?'

'Not much; I sent you in the next day...'

'To see what he revealed.'

'Exactly; but neither myself, Scicluna, or Prodi had anything to do with his murder. Concentrate on what I am saying, Thea. We allowed Debono to decide his own fate whilst still allowing you to do your job.'

'Prodi?'

'What?'

'Prodi; he's one of the Corsican Band of Brothers, too, then?'

'It is what it is, Thea.'

Spiteri stood and walked over to the office window. 'I don't know how to react to this, Kevin.'

'The night you confronted Tizian and the Sammuts, who told you where they were?'

'Cassar called me; he told me he couldn't get you.'

'I was right here, Thea. I knew when I didn't answer, he would panic and call you. Do you see now that this is how I how I meet my responsibilities? I light the path.'

'Yet Debono was still murdered; one of your brothers, Commissioner. What should be done about that? '

'If I were you, I would question Daniel Scippitto.'

'Who... Why... Who is he?'

'He is the brother of John Scippitto.'

Spiteri wracked her brain. 'John Scippitto, the guy who was murdered a few weeks back in Carradino, the guy who fitted the tampered meters?'

'The very same. You won't have to look far.'

'Why?'

'He's an inmate in Carradino, same floor as Debono, actually. He thinks Debono was behind his brother's killing. They are Maltese; family honour is important to them, too.'

Spiteri walked back to the commissioner's desk and sat down. 'What is wrong with all you people? You talk of honour as some sort of sheen of respectability to justify murder.'

'Justify, maybe. Maybe not, but it is an age-old reason.'

'Are there any other paths that you are going to enlighten me on today?'

'No.'

'What about Nicola Tizian; did he murder The Dahlia?'

'No.'

'How do you know?'

'Because if he did, I would have been told.'

'And what would you have done then, Kevin?'

'Like I said; I would have lit the path.'

***

Nicola Tizian ordered his yacht's captain to be ready to sail at eleven a.m. the following morning. He then informed all his managers that he wouldn't be round the units from today until further notice. In the meantime, they had to report to Franco and continue with the normal business banking arrangements.

He then called an unlisted number in Corsica: the call was answered, but without a greeting. Only Nicola Tizian spoke. 'It's shelved. Our honour is preserved.'

The Maltese Dahlia

Finally, Tizian called La Griza Restaurante in Valletta.

***

Kevin Galea anticipated that Spiteri was about to start asking some questions. 'A couple of final points, Thea. Firstly, I am very sorry about the tension between us in recent days and the difficult position I put you in. I hope that now you at least understand, if not fully agree or forgive. Finally, as from tomorrow, I will no longer be commissioner of *Pulizija*. Malta is moving on, and that is how it should be. As I said earlier, some people, like Debono, can't let go; but I can. In fact, I must. Jo Jo's body has started to reject the new heart. There is no hope. My dear wife has also found out that she has cancer. It is not at a critical stage, but my place is with them. Besides, the corridors of power need new people; people who know what honour really means. Thea, go on and leave now. All your investigations are completed. You need time to grieve Arrigo and, to be honest, it may be better to be out of sight in Floriana for a while. The Maltese Dahlia? Just as in USA, it will remain an open case; open but shelved indefinitely.'

Galea stood and held out his hand. 'Good-bye, Thea... and thank you.'

Spiteri refused the held-out hand; instead, she walked around the desk and embraced Kevin Galea. 'You do know the meaning of honour, Kevin. I'll miss you.' Spiteri wiped a tear from her eye before letting go of her proud, but defeated, friend. She closed the door quietly behind her as she left.

She decided that she was going to take Galea's advice and take a holiday. She went back to her office to let Said know what was happening and tidy up some remaining paperwork. As soon as she sat down at her desk, she noticed her voice mail light flashing; a two euro coin was sitting beside the phone along with other debris. *Eagle, I listen; map, I don't.*

EPILOGUE

Nicola Tizian was nervous and confused; perhaps even confused because he was nervous. He had never felt this anxiety over a woman before, or ever contemplated that any woman would refuse his invitation.

Thea Spiteri, too, was nervous. Six months ago, the idea of meeting a criminal for dinner in a romantic setting like La Griza would have been laughable; now Spiteri's views on right and wrong were in turmoil.

Tizian was charming, handsome, and polite... with an air of danger that Spiteri hated to admit she now found alluring.

Spiteri was regal, beautiful, and funny... with an air of uncertainty that Tizian found compelling.

The dinner wasn't over when Nicola Tizian stood up and walked around table and eased Thea Spiteri to her feet.

'Would you like to sail with me to Corsica tomorrow, Thea? Let me show you my homeland; maybe help you to understand.'

Spiteri looked into the eyes of this man who held such fire in his gaze. 'Was it you? Did you kill The Maltese Dahlia, Nicola?

'No, I swear, Thea. It wasn't me.'

'And Debono... and Abela... Why is death always around you, Nicola?'

'Thea, death is everywhere. Passion is not.'
Nicola Tizian leant forward and Thea Spiteri melted into his embrace.

***

The Dallas Morning News

Prominent Texas Surgeon Dies in Shark Attack
The prominent transplant surgeon, John "Duke" Wayne, originally from Texas, has been reported killed in a shark attack while apparently scuba diving in the Red Sea. Details are sketchy at the moment, but Doctor Wayne was apparently in Jeddah to check up on a patient there. Doctor Wayne had lately been working in Malta, but was believed to be seeking finance for a business venture he wished to pursue, most likely in the medical field.

Former friends and colleagues expressed surprise that Doctor Wayne had been scuba diving, as they had never known him to do so before. 'More of a movie type of guy, really,' one reportedly said.

More details to follow.

***

Another benefit of flying first class is that a passenger who wishes to work has plenty of space to do so.

The meticulous note taker in B2 had ticked off every box on his list apart from the last three. He hadn't liked to tempt fate, so he had decided to wait till he was on the plane. He took out his pen.

Remove duplicate Organ Search and Request Programme from Mater Dei system

Transfer 1 million euro to each of the Cayman Island Accounts

Decide final destination

The Maltese Dahlia

All ticked and closed. A degree in I.T. has its uses after all.

So I can't risk New York... Where to, where to... Decisions, decisions... Seattle, I think. I've never been there before. Sorry, Daphne.

I'll be successful there, as always, as I, Mauro Cali, I am The Messenger.

Paul Vincent Lee

Acknowledgments

As usual, I don't know either where to start, or where to finish, when it comes to acknowledging all the people who have helped in getting this book out there.

My family: I know for a fact that without them, I would not have survived the darkness. Thank you all.

Superintendant Antonello Grech of the Maltese *Pulizija*, Gozo for his insight into *Pulizija* procedures on the Maltese Islands. Much appreciated: any mistakes in the story are all mine.

The lovely Therese Gillies, Staff Midwife, Princess Royal Maternity Hospital, Glasgow... for all things "woman's bits."

Shane Watts, photographer par excellence at shanepwatts.com for supplying the photos for the book cover and my website.

Jes Darmanin from Storm Design for website development and Social Media work.

My editor, Susan Gottfried from West of Mars, for tireless and informative editing work

My cover designer: Jeanine Henning... what can I say... fantastic.

My layout and formatting guru... Katie Salidas... again, what can I say.

***

Finally, I feel it is important that I acknowledge the real life Black Dahlia—Elizabeth Short—whose horrific killing all those years ago still holds a fascination for many.

Elizabeth Short was not considered to be a prostitute, the closest reference being that she was a "good-time girl"—either way, her killing was barbaric.

Her killer was never caught nor, it appears, did he ever kill again. The case remains open.

About the Author

Follow Paul on: www.paulvincentlee.com , which also contains Paul's blog, It's Murder in Malta—where you can also join his e-mail list.

You can also follow Paul on Twitter: @LeeAuthor and Paul's Facebook page: Paul Vincent Lee Author

Paul can also be contacted by e-mail at: author@paulvincentlee.com

For Personal Appearance Requests, please contact: personalappearance@paulvincentlee.com

If you liked **The Maltese Orphans** *or* **The Maltese Dahlia:**

Hi, trying to earn a living as an independent writer is tough. Believe me, I know! The reason I've gotten this far is simple... It's YOU, the reader. If you have enjoyed any of my books, please take a few seconds to put a review on amazon.co.uk or amazon.com

A couple of lines can be all it takes to make a big difference.
Thank you.
Paul.

Keep in touch:
Contact me anytime! By email: author@paulvincentlee.com or on Twitter @LeeAuthor or through my Website: paulvincentlee.com
You can also sign up on my website if you would like to be emailed about future releases, including the next in The Thea Spiteri Series.

Gladiator
Troy
Midnight
By the Sea